THE LAND BEYOND
THE SEAS

Michael J. Lansdown

TSL Publications

First published in Great Britain in 2021
By TSL Publications, Rickmansworth

ISBN / 978-1-914245-49-7

Cover image by Bryn & Michael Lansdown

For

Caroline, Bryn, and Catrin

Acknowledgements

I would like to thank my friends at Watford Writers for their support, encouragement and patience during the writing of *The Land Beyond the Seas*. Special thanks to Helen, Pat, David, and Brian for their eagle-eyed reading of the drafts and for their excellent observations and suggestions.

The story so far . . .

Two years earlier, fifteen-year-old convict William Parker arrived in Australia, having been found guilty of the murder of Adam Clarke, the son of his boss, canal owner Edmund Clarke. By a stroke of good fortune, the fatal fight on the canal side had been seen by one of Mr Clarke's footmen who then testified that William had attacked Adam only as an act of self-defence. As a result, and amid dramatic scenes at Hertford Assizes, the judge commuted the death sentence to one of fourteen years' transportation to New South Wales, the new penal colony "beyond the seas".

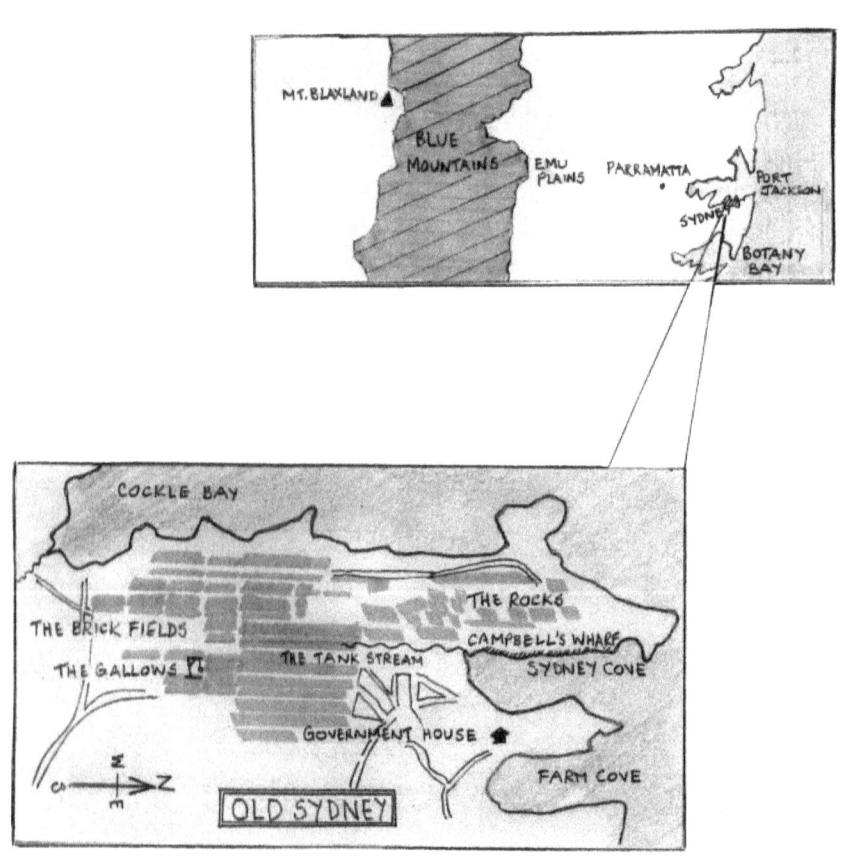

MT. BLAXLAND

BLUE MOUNTAINS

EMU PLAINS

PARRAMATTA

PORT JACKSON

SYDNEY

BOTANY BAY

COCKLE BAY

THE ROCKS

THE BRICK FIELDS

CAMPBELL'S WHARF

THE GALLOWS

THE TANK STREAM

SYDNEY COVE

GOVERNMENT HOUSE

FARM COVE

OLD SYDNEY

New South Wales and Sydney

ca 1810

Part 1

Christmas 1803

Near Port Jackson, New South Wales

1

"Move, Parker, and you're a dead man."

William lay, spread-eagled; the hot, red soil burning his face.

"On your knees," said the voice – the accent, London, a familiar one – "and don't go trying any funny business or I'll be forced to use this." William felt the end of a gun barrel stabbing at the base of his skull.

The boot on his neck lifted and William coughed, spat into the earth, then turned to look at his captor... *yes, it was Sergeant Smith.* A trickle of blood ran from his forehead and he let it run, knowing that any sudden movement could be his last. He straightened up, slowly, hands aloft. The game was over.

A little way off, a horse neighed and stamped at the ground, impatient to be heading home.

The soldier, backing off, gestured that William should move towards a rough canvas bag, lying nearby. A loop of rope poked out of the opening at the top.

"That's it – on your feet – slowly. Pick up the rope and put your 'ands behind your back. Gently now, don't get no silly ideas. Now, turn away."

William allowed the sergeant to push his hands through the loop, felt it tighten, then stumbled forwards as he was pushed up the dusty side of the dry riverbed where he had spent the night, out onto the open plain. The rope bit deep into his wrists, and his shoulders jarred, but it was the injustice that hurt him most. The rope slackened as Smith mounted his horse and gave its flanks a sharp kick. It tossed its head and started a slow walk. It knew it was a long way back to camp.

"Right, now it's *prisoner* Parker again, and don't you forget it," said Smith. "So, just keep on walking, and don't stop till I tells you."

William said nothing and did just as the soldier ordered. One foot in front of the other, kicking up the dust with every tired step. Through the haze, three hundred yards ahead, he could make out the small, lean figure of a native leading the way – occasionally stopping, gesturing, making sure the two *duggeri-gai* and their strange beast were keeping to the right direction.

The day wore on, the sun now reaching its zenith. William heard the slurp of Smith taking a drink and stopped to look round. Parched, and barely able to form the words, he addressed his captor: "If you're going to get your reward, you're going to have to keep me alive."

Smith looked down at him, askance. "Don't you go trying to tell me my bloody job, son. I couldn't give a tinker's cuss if you live or you die." He took another swig, "But as I've come all this way…" He directed a thin stream of water towards his prisoner, and William struggled to capture every last drop of the life-saving liquid. *Waste not, want not, Will.* His mother's words came flooding back to him across the years, crossing the vastness of the oceans that now separated them. He turned his head as the flow finally threatened to drown him and, abject as he was, he could not help but see the dark humour of this eventuality: drowning in the desert. What a stupid way to die, after months of refusing to go under.

The following hours were a blur of sun, thirst and flies, Smith giving him regular sips of water – enough to keep him walking – as a prisoner brought back alive was worth something. A dead one, on the other hand, would indeed be a criminal waste; a waste of all the hours, days, and months gone into bringing him half way round the world, to this land beyond the seas. The soldier, bored by hours of his own company, made another effort at conversation as William shuffled along in silence.

"So, you didn't get to *China* then Parker?" the soldier mocked. "None of them ever does. The sun or snakes usually gets them. Then it's the dingoes. Surprised you survived this long to tell the truth."

William stared at his feet and winced at the memory of the things he had seen: bleached bones; fluttering rags; the scattered remnants of what few possessions the fools were carrying before their spirits finally joined the others in what the natives called The Dreamtime. And the skulls, with their broken grins and empty sockets. He would never forget the skulls.

"The Captain won't be too happy. Ever had a floggin'?"

William said nothing. What was there to say? The man was right. No one ever got away. Those who tried, came back in a box – unless the dogs got them first, in which case the coffin could be saved; until the next time...

Sometime later, Smith tried again.

"Can't understand it me'self. You keep your 'ead down, does your work alright. Could make something of yourself once you've done your time. And who's that tart, that admirer of yours – Toft, Mary Toft ain't it? Be quick or the likes of Tommy Gates and his crew will get in there before you, son. Well, you'd have to be crazy to leave *her* behind."

William closed his eyes and tried to block her face from appearing. Sometimes, he thought that maybe he *was* going crazy. The events of the previous two years had certainly been a madness of sorts. But the pain in his feet and the dryness of his throat told him that not everything was in his head.

"Don't say much do you Parker? S'ppose you want to forget yer criminal past. Murder by drowning, wasn't it? Your boss's son *in his father's own bloody canal* from what I 'eard." Smith shook his head and started to laugh. "Can see why you weren't too popular!"

"He was *rich* and I was *poor*," William blurted out, as if this explained everything. "Who were they going to believe? We dug the canal, but he *owned* it!"

"Oh...so, you got sent out here – fourteen-year stretch?"

William looked down at his feet again. "That's right. I thought I was going to swing."

"Quite a story, Parker," said the soldier, "And you're one of the lucky bastards. There's others here who done nothin' more than steal a leg of lamb, or a rich man's 'andkerchief. Let alone kill their boss's son and heir."

Neither spoke again until they reached a small clump of vegetation where Smith announced they would stop for the night. Within the circle of trees lay a shallow pool, a billabong, where he led the horse, allowing it to water. A short way off was a small area of flattened ground, sheltering in the lee of a sandstone rock the size of William's childhood cottage. A rough patch of scorched earth attested to the fact that others had been there before, but the soldier, following a cursory inspection, confirmed that whoever it had been was now long gone, so they should not be expecting visitors that night.

Smith untied William's hands and pointed at the trees, then sat down. "Final job before we eat. Build us a fire. And remember – no funny business," he said, patting the gun lying across his legs. William nodded and started to collect whatever branches or loose bark he could find strewn upon the ground. Meanwhile, the fourth member of their party busied himself, digging up the roots that would be their evening meal. A short time later, the tinder, dry and infused with resin, sparked easily into life, baking the wild parsnips and warding off any wildlife inclined to join them for dinner.

After they had eaten, the sky began its metamorphosis from bright blue, to red, and then to the deepest of blacks. As the temperature dropped, both men laid back and stared at the stars. Apart from the occasional crack of a twig exploding into flame, or the far-off call of a night animal, it was as peaceful a place as William could recall, the dark beauty unlike anything he could remember from his previous life, in England. A billion stars filled the space between the treetops, the darkest of canopies bedecked with the brightest pinpoints of blue-white light.

"Oi! Parker. I said, how come you didn't swing?"

William jumped, brought back to earth by the voice from the void.

"Hurry up and tell me; I wants to know."

William sighed, and spoke to the darkness.

"It was a servant – the butler I think – he'd seen it all. Seen the fight. He came to the courtroom and, well, saved my life I suppose. He told them what really happened. He saved me from the rope."

He heard Smith snort, unseen.

"Like I said, you're a lucky bastard. Right, time to sleep…oh, and just in case you have any stupid ideas, the black fellah's got the ears and the eyes of a cat. And he's under strict orders to let you 'ave it in the back if you tries to bolt again. Understood? Now, get some shut-eye. It'll be a long day tomorrow."

The next morning the pair woke early. The sun chased away the chill of the night, and after a quick breakfast they adopted their now familiar positions, one atop and one alongside the horse, and continued their steady journey eastwards. The tracker led the way. They saw little of interest, and spoke even less, as the mounting heat of the day made every step, every breath, an effort of will for horse and convict alike. Even Sergeant Smith, sitting comfortably astride his old friend, wiped the sweat from his brow and squinted into the distance, searching for those familiar landmarks that would bring them home once more.

Just before sunset, the guide shouted once and William spotted the unmistakable lines of the colony: the convicts' cottages, the white sails of the windmills, the tall masts of the ships at dock, and he knew that all was lost – for the time-being, at least. To try to escape now *would* be mad; he had no choice but to return, face the music, and take his punishment…like a man. He had seen floggings before and felt his legs almost buckle beneath him with the memory. But somehow, he would survive.

They had taken his life away once.

They would not take it again.

2

Not for the first time in his short life, William was forced to meet the cold stare of authority. Then, it had been the rheumy eyes of Judge Samuels, sentencing him to death by hanging, transmuted to transportation to His Majesty's colony overseas. Now, as he stood before the Captain, he tried to keep his chin up, his gaze level.

"Parker," said Captain Faulks unsmiling. "It's some time since I heard that name. So, to what do I owe the pleasure?"

He studied a piece of paper in his hand.

"Ah, '*Escaped overnight whilst part of a bush-clearing gang*.'" He looked up. "You do know what we do to bolters, don't you? So, what have you got to say for yourself?"

William straightened his shoulders and cleared his throat before replying.

"I have little new to say, Sir, but if I may, I will say it again. I am innocent of the crime of murder. I love and miss my family, and, though she spat me out, my country. I fear the lash, Sir, but fear my Lord and maker more; and I truly believe that He would not forgive me if I were *not* to stand up for what I believe is right. Sir."

The captain half stood then leaned across his desk. He was a man of average size but of huge reputation; William fought against the urge to take a backwards step.

The captain fixed William where he stood, his gaze unwavering.

"What you say you may, or may not, have done is of little concern to me." A sweep of his arm took in the camp that surrounded them. "There is not a man, nor woman, amongst you that does not plead his or her innocence. Not one has stolen, stabbed, or bludgeoned their neighbour, or assaulted a man who was guilty of nothing more than being their better. No one has poached their master's rabbits. Not a *single* person is guilty of smashing their employer's machinery." He stood and walked towards the window then, warming to his theme, turned suddenly to face William. "No! All the evidence is total fabrication, a tissue of lies woven by those with nothing better to do than spend their time sending good men and women halfway around the globe...and for what? Well, young Parker, tell me, do: who is it then that steals, murders and destroys, if they are not to be found among the reeking ranks of you and your fellow prisoners?"

He walked back to his desk, sat, and steepled his fingers, his head cocked in anticipation.

William cleared his throat again before answering.

"Sir, in this world there are those that have, and there are those that have not. Those that *have* make the rules, the laws, that keep us, the *have nots*, in our place." He stopped briefly and met the captain's eyes. "We cannot condemn the man who steals a loaf of bread to feed his starving child, or the servant girl whose fingers cannot resist the feel of her mistress's lace. Nor the child who knows no home or the warmth of a parent's love, and steals a handkerchief from a gentleman who owns a thousand more besides. For the murderers and men of violence I do not speak, but each and every one of them perhaps, has their story: if only you would listen." And then he stopped, and looked at the floor.

For a full minute the captain said nothing, then looked to Sergeant Smith, waving at him to take the prisoner outside. William, his feet and hands shackled, shuffled to the door, and waited outside.

"Close the door, Smith," the captain said, then made his way to the window from where he was able to survey the scene below. Gangs of convicts, mainly men and boys, marched in lines, across an untidy, busy landscape. In several places, prisoners were hard at it, clearing stands of trees and cutting back the thick bush which daily threatened to claim back the land from which it had been hacked. Elsewhere, under the constant glare of uniformed guards, men in groups were wielding axes and hammers, building shelters for the colony's growing population. Groups of females too, young girls and older women doing their bit for the life of the camp, drew the captain's eye: washing, cleaning or tending to the animals of the prison farm – it was a scene of honest endeavour, he thought, where some good at least could come from the bad that had been their former lives.

"Stand at ease, Sergeant. Tell me, what sort of prisoner is Parker?"

"Parker? One of the quieter ones. Likes to keep 'imself to 'imself, Sir. Never caused any trouble, but you can tell 'e's angry. 'E don't like being 'ere."

"Mmm," the captain mused, "and what's he like as a worker – when he's assigned a task and is made to do it?"

"One of the best, Sir. And 'e's an 'ard worker. Strong and intelligent, and I think 'e can read a little."

"Indeed. Interesting, even if he has not much use for reading and writing here in the bush."

"And," the soldier added with a note of admiration, "'e's got a way with the animals, Sir. Never known anyone who can calm an 'orse the way 'e can. Sort of just breathes on 'em and they quieten down. Sir."

"Do you like him, soldier?"

"Don't *like* any of the effin' vermin, beggin' your pardon Sir, but as vermin go 'e's one of the better ones. 'E's got what I think you might call, '*potential*.'"

"Indeed. Thank you soldier. Bring him back in."

William returned to the cool of the office, his eyes taking a moment to readjust to the shadows in which the captain stood, hands clasped behind his back.

"Parker. I have taken some time to think about what I should do with you. You know that for attempting to escape there can be only one punishment, so you *will* feel the sting of the lash before the day is through. However, I am satisfied that you may make something of your life if only you allow yourself the opportunity to better your condition. Therefore, on this occasion, and on this occasion only, I will limit the punishment to 50 lashes of the Cat. And on recovering, Parker, I expect you to repay my trust and mercy by directing your abilities and talents – you have a way with horses, I believe – to the betterment of the camp and your fellow prisoners. Do I make myself understood?"

William said nothing but made a small bow of the head to show that he followed the captain's meaning.

"Take him away Sergeant, and arrange for the punishment to take place before sunset."

As William was led away the captain poured himself a large sherry from the crystal decanter that he kept close-by: to help him through the day.

The urgent clanking of the bell told prisoners that they were to assemble below the captain's hut, and in their scores, they trudged wearily towards the spot where a large wooden frame stood waiting. The Triangle was as familiar to the residents of the colony as were the water-pump or village cross in happier times – in happier places. From every part of the camp they came: men, women, children, soldiers and their superiors. Few were excused the spectacle of a flogging, a lesson to all would-be bolters, both old and young.

Forming a rough semi-circle, they waited for the door of the captain's hut to open. The Irish whispered darkly in their own tongue whilst others, Tommy Gates and his friends amongst them, shuffled their feet and craned their necks, waiting for the spectacle to begin. At long last, the captain appeared in full military regalia, and stood upon the veranda high above them. As he emerged, a small band of guards broke through the crowd, shepherding William, who was to be the sad centre of attention, in chains before them. He stood, hard-faced, in front of the triangular frame and looked beyond the heads of the crowd to a distant line of eucalyptus trees, on the other side of which he had been captured. Prisoners looked on mutely – resignation, fascination, and dread combining in equal parts. Almost everyone had heard and seen all this before: the grand speech from the captain; the message that God loves us, but that it is sometimes necessary to punish in order to keep His children on the straight and narrow; that those who obeyed His laws and those of His Majesty, King George, had nothing to fear; then, the dread and bravery in the eyes of the wretch tied to The Triangle, the crack of the whip, the cloying smell of blood.

"Prisoners, I have called you here today to witness the flogging of William Parker, one of your own. Parker made the foolish, and ultimately futile decision, to attempt an escape and was caught and brought back to camp. Fortunately for him, we might say, as those who leave here unlawfully are normally brought back in a box, if the dingoes haven't yet had their fill.

"I say to you all, to attempt an escape is to invite a lingering death. There is *no* safe haven beyond the mountains, no China, of silks and exotic perfumes, as some of you are deluded enough to believe. It is a wilderness like unto which Christ himself was cast, to be lost for forty days and forty nights. But here, there will be no Divine Father to look over you and scoop you up to safety. No manna from heaven scattered upon the earth. Instead, your reward will be a slow, painful death by starvation and thirst, or the sharp sting of the serpent which you will surely welcome to end your miserable days."

A number of prisoners took their eyes off the Captain, inviting a cuff around the head or the sharp prod of a musket barrel by a nearby guard. But one small prisoner stared steadfastly ahead. She bit her lip and tightly clenched her fists, defying the tears that were starting to prick her eyes. Mary Toft had never known real love, neither as a child nor as the young woman she now was. But what she felt for William as he leant against the frame, his bare back bathed in the soft light of the setting sun, was as close as she had ever come to loving another person. She thought back to the time before they arrived in New South Wales: no words had been said at the time, but she had noticed the young man, with his dark good looks and faraway eyes, as they awaited trial, and then again when they finally left the ship which brought them across the oceans. In the following months, their paths had rarely crossed, but on the few occasions when they were able to converse, they had done so, she talking thirteen to the dozen, he listening intently, hardly able to get a word in. She allowed herself a wistful smile, then bit down harder as the captain spoke again.

"Sergeant Gordon, you may now administer the punishment. Fifty lashes. Batches of ten."

She looked around momentarily and caught Gates looking in her direction, then turned away and watched as the soldier held the whip in his right hand and smoothed the nine strands with his left so that the knotted ends lined up neatly – like infantrymen, she thought, ready to attack. Hooking his arm far behind his head, he brought the Cat down hard on William's back, leaving an angry red weal across his shoulders; Mary held her breath. Some looked away, but fixing her eyes on those of William she willed him to sustain whatever punishment he would have to endure. He flinched but kept his silence as the second stroke broke the skin and a trickle of blood started its slow journey from his shoulders, down his spine and onto his breeches. The third opened up a red gash where his collar would normally be, and William jerked his head back, gritting his teeth. Mary, all the while, willed him to be strong, feeling every stroke almost as keenly as he, absorbing the pain as if by sharing it she could somehow halve the agony. With each blow, she fought back the scream that threatened to explode from her breast, and by the time the punishment reached its awful conclusion, her lip too ran with blood.

It was two days later when William finally woke up. He felt his eyelids open then shut again, the daylight filtering through the window too bright for his fevered brain. His back burned and his throat was parched, his whole world like a furnace.

"Water," he heard himself say, his voice barely audible, then felt the cool of a cup pressing his cracked lips gently apart. The liquid found its way into his mouth, and onto his chin, making him splutter as his throat struggled to accept it. He tried to sit up, then felt a soft hand pressing him back onto the bed.

"Shh, lie still William," a voice, familiar yet distant, soothed him as he lay. From somewhere, he thought he could hear the everyday sounds of men arguing, the clank of a hammer on an anvil, and the voice of a girl singing – sweet, but, oh, so far away.

Sometime later, he woke again with a start; his brow felt cool and wet. Someone was sitting at his side.

"Mary? Is it you? What happened? Where am I?"

She squeezed his hand.

"Of course it's me, William Parker. Don't try to sit yet. You had a brush with the Cat, but you're safe now. You are in the hospital block, Will. You've been asleep for nearly two days – a fever. We thought we'd lost you, but you are past the worst and now we need to look after your back."

At this, William felt the fire behind him and tried to roll onto his side.

"William. Lie still. You have to let the lotions do their work. I know it hurts, but it's for the best."

William groaned.

"How long have I been here?"

"Two days. I just told you, Will. Now close your eyes and rest a while. You've got to get your strength back."

William managed a small nod.

"Yes, Mary," he whispered, then drifted off to sleep again.

3

William was digging, then stopped to lean a moment on his shovel. It had been several months since the flogging and he was thinking of Mary – how her soft hands and sweet words had soothed him back to life. The scars were still raw and he pushed his shoulders together gently in a bid to ease the pain; then, letting out a long, slow, breath, he squinted towards the distant hills, asking himself when it would all end.

"Parker! Stop yer daydreaming boy, and put yer bloody back into it!"

The cruel irony of Corporal Marks' words was not lost on William. He snapped to attention, and when he looked round, he knew – what he had long suspected – that he was being watched, and not by the soldiers alone. Earlier, he thought he had noticed the stares of the convict he knew only as The Big Fellah, and now, with the trace of a smile and a nod in his direction, the other convict had confirmed it was true. A huge man, with a wild and angry look, he cleared the roots and branches as if they were playthings. What for William and his fellow convicts was a morning's work, The Big Fellah would do single-handedly, and in half the time too. And now, for reasons unknown to him, William seemed to have become the unwanted focus of the big man's attention. He looked down again and continued to dig at the roots of the gum tree he had been working on since dawn.

An hour later, on a whistle, the men stopped and stood still, waiting for permission to take a short break. On hearing the word, they dropped their tools and moved to find the nearest log or flat rock on which they could rest. Some sat with heads bowed and eyes closed, their fingers intertwined as if in prayer. Some, indeed, did lose themselves in prayer, whilst others thought of nothing but sleep or their next meal.

William sat on a fallen bough at the edge of the clearing, closed his eyes and listened to the constant din of the bush. He listened intently, surrendering himself to the buzz of insects, the startled call of exotic birds, and the harsh bark of soldiers that seemed to echo through the forest from morn till night.

"Englishman. What's yer name?"

William jumped, sensing the size of the man before he saw him. He was standing over him.

"Parker. William Parker. Who wants to know?" he answered.

The visitor sat without speaking and, as he looked deep into the forest, hummed a plaintive air. His fingers fiddled with a piece of brush that had stuck to his breeches, and William noted the huge hands and the delicate way the fingers manipulated the stem into a variety of shapes and knots. This continued for some time until he spoke again.

"Are ye afraid of me, William Parker? Most men are."

"Do I have cause to fear you, Mr…?"

"O'Connor. Patrick O'Connor," he cut in. "Or some call me The Big Fellah. Ye can take yer choice."

"I know nothing of you, Mr O'Connor."

"They call me The Big Fellah, not just on account of me size, Mr Parker," he continued. "I'm big cos I'm the fellah who every-one looks up to. The Boss, The Gaffer, The Top of the Heap, you might say. Do you have a problem with that?"

William shuffled on his log, avoiding O'Connor's gaze.

"I have no problem with that Mr O'Connor. I keep myself to myself. With the Redcoats watching our every move I have no need of additional enemies in this place. We all must survive, and each one of us has his own way of doing that."

"Ah, wise words Mr Parker, wise words," said O'Connor nod-ding, then made himself more comfortable. The log shifted and William was forced to use his hands to stop himself tumbling to the ground.

"You see. Getting on with me is easy…as easy as falling off a log! Isn't that what the English say, William Parker? Never a truer word was spoken in your language or in mine."

William sensed a thin smile beneath the beard but said nothing, uneasy at this strange and uninvited intrusion on his rest-time.

The two sat in silence, one looking into the forest, the other at the ground, until a second whistle signalled the re-commencement of work.

The Irishman struggled to his feet. "It's been good to make your acquaintance, Mr Parker," he said, then slapped him on the shoul-der, winking as William fought the sudden bolt of pain surging across his back. O'Connor moved off and returned to the group of men he had been working with, several of whom touched their caps deferentially, moving out of the way as he approached – like ducks before a barge. William thought he heard him say something to the others in words he could not understand, then felt the stare of many more pairs of eyes watching him as he made his way back to his shovel, and the comfort of his work station.

It was about three weeks after O'Connor's first approach. William again sat apart from his work gang, daydreaming. His thoughts were mainly of Mary, of the way she smiled and pushed the hair from her face; of his childhood, of Hensford and his time on the canal…when the sun shone every day and his father would take him into the fields to look for rabbits and –

"Parker! Can you not *hear* me?"

William woke abruptly to find O'Connor's eyes on him, fixed and staring, from beneath his heavy brow.

"I've been saying your feckin' name for minutes now. Ye wouldn't be tryin' to ignore me now, would ye Parker?"

William sighed, resigned. O'Connor cocked his head and signalled that he should move up the log; come closer. William did as he was asked, but turned again, avoiding the big man's stare.

"That's better. Let's try to be civil, English."

The last word, O'Connor said with a dark note, any hint at bonhomie buried deep and hidden, like an axe in rotten wood.

"I have a proposition," he said. This time his voice was like that of an anxious churchgoer, keen not to be overheard, and his eyes scanned the clearing for signs that any other member of the "congregation" might be listening. Convicts were sitting, chatting, or lying down, grabbing a few moments of shut-eye. The half-dozen soldiers nearby passed round a pipe of rough tobacco. Nobody was listening. The conversation continued.

"A proposition? What sort of *proposition*, Mr O'Connor?" William whispered back.

O'Connor shuffled his feet, like a nervous child. Then wringing his hands together, looked around, checking again that they could not be heard.

"I need to get out of this festerin' hole, 'cos if I don't I will surely die," he said, his voice dropping, his tone almost confessional.

William said nothing in reply. This was a sentiment expressed daily by every man jack of them and added nothing to his understanding of the other man's proposal.

"Now *you*, William Parker," O'Connor continued quietly, "you *did* get away, and further than most. I have heard it said that you lasted four long days out there in the bush, saw things that no other man in the camp, save the guards, has seen. You were a *dead* man, finished, eaten by dingoes, but you come back, alive. You've seen what lies beyond the horizon, and you could be useful to get to know," he tried to catch William's eye, "if you follow my drift."

A soldier coughing on his pipe made William start as he began to understand the interest O'Connor now had in him. He thought before speaking.

"Mr O'Connor. What you say is true, but you are still talking in riddles. What is it you propose? That I assume the position of a school-master, maybe? Deliver an evening lesson to you and your friends?"

O'Connor allowed himself a small, sardonic laugh and carefully studied a spot on the ground a little way in front of his feet.

"Ah, now that would be a grand thing for all of us to see, would it not? An Englishman in his pulpit, granting us Paddies the wisdom of his vast experience. T'would be the shortest lesson of all time – and pearls before swine, no doubt!" he said, then turned to look at William directly.

"Well, *what?* Mr O'Connor," said William, and felt his anger starting to rise.

But before O'Connor was able to answer, the whistle blew and a soldier's shout rang through the forest, ordering them back to work.

As their paths crossed, William whispered a final question. "And what's in it for me if I help you, Mr O'Connor?"

The big man bent close as if to adjust his boot-lace, so close that William felt the heat of his body. "More's a case of what's in it for you if you don't, Mr Parker; if you *don't*."

Then he heaved himself up and started across the clearing

Turning once, he raised his spade. "For King and Country," he smiled.

William waited.

In the allotted place, at the allotted time: The Big Fellah's threats echoing in his ears.

The forest was dark and quiet, the only sounds coming from the huts and campfires a few minutes distant from where he stood, alone.

The crack of a twig made him start.

"O'Connor?" he whispered.

Nothing.

"*O'Connor!* Is that you?"

A huge hand gripped his shoulder.

"English, calm yerself." O'Connor was speaking low. "There's just the two of us."

William felt his body tense, then took a step away from the looming figure, silhouetted, dark against the moon.

"Come," said O'Connor, "let's find ourselves a log to sit on – somewhere comfortable where we can have our little chat."

"*Little chat?* What do you want of me O'Connor? And why did you threaten me so, if I did not turn up?"

"Ah, now I wouldn't be after calling it a threat, Mr Parker. More of a...an *inducement*. A little persuasion goes a long way, as they say."

William allowed O'Connor to shepherd him to the trunk of a fallen eucalyptus, its bark littering the ground like parchment. He sat and waited for O'Connor to begin talking, to illuminate him, in this, the darkest of the camp's many dark corners.

"Well, it's like this," started O'Connor, his tone like that of an exhausted parent explaining himself again to a child. "I am an

O'Connor, from the village of Baile Conaola, in the county of Donegal…in Ireland," he added, unnecessarily. "I am a hard man, brought up on a diet of tatties and water, and by the time I was thirteen I had helped bury my brothers, all five of them. And my father, the lazy bastard, but not before he had pissed the family fortune, such as it was, up against the wall of the nearest inn. I have had to fight all my life, English. When your countrymen came to my village they called us *rebels* – the first word I learned of the King's English – and that is what I have been all my life since: a rebel. So, you see, Mr Parker, I am not a mule, and I won't do another man's bidding against my wishes – not for stick and not for carrot. I am one of nature's free spirits, you could say, but here, in this feckin' shit-hole, I am not. I need to escape, get away from the camp; and you, Englishman, hold the key."

William sat, unmoving, unsure of how he should respond, the silence crowding in on him with every empty second.

"Do you not wish to know what the mad oul' fellah is on about?" he heard O'Connor say, the amazement clear in his voice.

"If I *do* hold the key," William cut in, "would I be here still, sitting with you, in a prison? When I could be a free man, a hundred miles away?"

"You have a point, I'll concede," said O'Connor, and nodded. "The thing is that you *do* have the key, but you choose not to use it. The *key* is what you have in your head – the facts, the information, everything about the bush that you alone know. You have it, but have chosen to guard it jealously which, if you don't mind me saying, Mr Parker, seems a tad ungenerous of you."

Beneath the smooth words and easy manner, William sensed O'Connor's frustration churning, his anger building. O'Connor was the camp newcomer whose reputation for violence had spread like wildfire through the bush and was already common knowledge. William took a deep breath and turned to face him.

"Mr O'Connor, what you need to understand – what you *must* understand – is that I did not make it to freedom. I am a failure, and I have the scars on my back to prove it."

"I understand. Now carry on. Tell me what you know and start from the beginning," came the cold reply.

"Very well." William sighed and closed his eyes, concentrating hard, as he tried to recall the details of those early terrifying minutes. "I left the camp going east – by the Government House. Nobody would expect me to take that route. I passed the stables and made my way down towards the coast at the Cove."

"Farm Cove?"

"Yes, Farm Cove, then headed south, with the sea at my back."

William paused, thought he heard the crash of the waves, then carried on.

"Here you must be careful of soldiers – even at night. Mr Palmer's brickworks are nearby – keep them on your right – and remember, the militia are there in numbers. Then I walked towards the south, keeping the sound of the sea on my left, until, I don't know, until the start of daylight."

He stopped and stared into the darkness, trying to remember.

"I rested a while, then decided to walk west, the long shadows pointing the way."

"West you say?" O'Connor's voice came from the blackness.

"Yes, that's right. Follow the shadows in the morning – they are your friends. The rest of the day, I kept as close as I could to the trees, avoiding open spaces and resting when I felt exhausted. And water, water is scarce – you need to take supplies. There are few animals at this point too, although I did hear the barking of the wild dogs. And beware spotted snakes: the red bellied blacks – they live amongst the brush. One bite and your journey is over. And then I just walked and walked, until I was too exhausted to go any further."

"Did you not sleep?"

William gave a quiet laugh. "I did, but not by choice. I found myself a sheltered spot and cleared the ground of stones as best I could, but I would have slept on solid rock. The next day I kept on heading west. Between the stands of gumtrees, in the distance, you can just make out the blue of the hills. Make this your goal. At some point, I cannot remember when, I came to a stream and filled my bottle. You must do the same as the land now becomes more open, and drier still. You will see the bodies of dead animals – kangaroos mostly, and…" William hesitated, "those that never made it any further."

He stopped speaking and closed his eyes tight, but still saw the grins and the empty stares of convict skulls before him.

"Go on, Parker, what then?" said O'Connor, "I cannot write, but my memory is fierce."

William opened his eyes, and sighed again. "I slept the night and the next day was captured," he said simply. "And that, Mr O'Connor, is as much as I can tell you. I have no more to say – except," he paused, "except to state that I do not believe that China lies beyond the hills, and that anyone who does, is as good as dead before he even starts."

"And that is it?"

"Yes; that's it," said William, finally, then felt O'Connor stand up.

"So now, Mr Parker, I'll take my leave of you, and I'll go back and speak to my men. And I pray, for your sake, that what you have told me is true."

William felt the rank warmth of his breath on his face.

"You take care now, getting home."

4

"Parker! Come with me."

William left the line of convicts, queueing for their morning duties, and shuffled over, hands thrust deep in his pockets, to where Sergeant Smith was waiting. His heart started pounding, his head still filled with the words from The Big Fellah's night-time meeting.

"Sarge? Have I done something wrong?"

"Not as far as I know. Have you?" The sergeant looked at him enquiringly.

William shook his head and followed the soldier as he led the way towards the stables, built in the long shadows of Government House.

"The captain said you should spend more time with the 'orses. I put in a word," he said, and gave William a knowing smile. "Got to be better than breakin' yer back with an axe or a shovel."

William returned the smile, and nothing more was said until they came to where the horses were housed overnight. The sergeant stopped at the entrance and gestured to a soldier in shirtsleeves, his red jacket hanging from the stable door.

"Corporal James here will tell you what to do, Parker."

The soldier stopped what he was doing and came over to the door.

"Make good use of him, Taffy, he's got a way with the animals."

As the sergeant departed, William whispered, "Thank you sarge; it's appreciated," the sergeant giving a hint of a nod in response.

"Right, Parker is it?" said the corporal.

"Yes, Sir."

"What d'you know about this lot?" he said, slapping the flanks of an ageing mare. "Apart from the four legs and the piles of 'orse-shit."

"I was brought up with them, Sir – canal horses, mostly. I was in charge of a dozen of them – fed them, groomed them, led them to and from the workings, treated them when they were sick. There's not much I don't know about them."

The corporal raised an eyebrow then spat onto the hay-strewn floor.

"Well, that's good then, isn't it? Get this one ready for a day at the brickfields – ten minutes you've got."

"Sir!"

As soon as he was alone William slipped in beside the horse and, seeing a roughly chalked sign, learned that her name was Argent. The horse turned its head and eyed William, wary of this uninvited newcomer. William whispered the name into its ear, running his hand over its forelock, along its nose and down to its muzzle. The horse raised its large grey head and shook it a few times, then seemed to relax in his company.

"Good girl – now let's try you with this," he said, gently slipping the bridle into place. William sensed a token resistance but secured the rest of the tack with little difficulty.

"Good girl, Argent, we're friends already."

As promised, a few minutes later Corporal James returned to find William and the horse ready for work.

"Very good, Parker. Argent 'ere can be a bit of an 'andful when she wants to be. Right, let's get goin', let's get to work. It's to the brickfields we're off."

William led Argent out and joined the other horses and their handlers. As they crossed the open ground, William caught the figure of someone calling to him from the banks of the Tank Stream – it was Mary – and he half-raised his hand in response. Inwardly, he was beaming.

A short time later, they came to Cockle Creek. William scanned the scene before him, a wide expanse of clay and mud, criss-crossed by a network of small interconnected streams, noiselessly emptying into the murky waters of the creek itself. Everywhere he looked, he saw men digging out the raw clay, forming it into piles, ready for the horses and bullock carts to take it to one of a dozen buildings in nearby Brickfield Village. William helped hitch the horse to a simple sled used to drag the clay from creek to kiln, whilst bullock carts trundled by, doing the same job, but on a bigger scale. The corporal sauntered over to where William waited for further orders.

"Right, now that you're set, join that lot over there, Parker. Help load the clay onto the drag, then follow the rest – the animals know where to go."

"Yes Sir," said William, and led Argent over to where a handful of convicts were knee deep in water, shovelling the thick red clay onto the banks of the creek. As he looked around him, the same small scene was repeated over and over – three or four men standing in water, shovels and adzes lifting, then falling, the drawn-out squelch of clay refusing to budge, then the wet slap as it finally joined the growing mound.

"Don't just stand there staring, mate, put your bloody back into it. It don't move by itself!" A voice from below brought him back to the moment.

William quickly picked up a shovel and started loading the clay onto the sled, piling it up until it started to ooze back onto the slimy ground.

"That's enough, mate," the man in the channel shouted. "Now bugger off to the kilns – and don't 'ang about or we'll all cop it. Work steady, work as a team," he added before driving his shovel again deep into the clay. William saluted, then led Argent on the short walk to the village.

This was to form the pattern for the day: load the drag, ten-minute walk to the village, unload the drag, five-minute walk to the clay, load the drag, and so on, and so on…until told to stop by one of the men in red. It transported him to his time as a boy, helping his father and his team of navvies build the canal – the Hensford Arm of the canal, at least. Here, apart from the shouting, nobody really spoke, so William found time to daydream, now and again breaking the silence, an odd word exchanged with his new four-footed friend. And his daydreams today seemed always to return to the same thing – Mary: how Mary had nursed him back to health, Mary and their snatched conversations, Mary standing, hands on hips…and the kiss blown on the wind earlier in the day. Mary? A kiss? Had he imagined it?

The afternoon wore on, and as the air cooled the men in the holes stopped digging and started to climb back onto "dry land". There had been no whistle, no clanking of bells, just a recognition by soldiers and convicts alike that this was the end of the day. The place worked like clockwork, and the clock said home-time. Scores of mud-soaked convicts and their overseers, accompanied by horses and teams of oxen, made their way wearily homewards. William yawned and cleaned his hands on his breeches, barely able to find a patch that was not already caked in cloying mud.

"Good day, was it Parker?"

Corporal James had caught him unawares, smiling at the thought of Mary.

"Yes, Corporal. I was back to being a mudlark."

The soldier narrowed his eyes.

"Just make sure you don't enjoy it too much Parker, or we might send you back to chopping logs."

William nodded, and trudged back to the stables.

Later that evening, William made his way to the canteen. He'd managed to clean most of the mud from his clothes and his breeches were now drying as he walked. Collecting his rations, he sat at one of the benches and started to eat his food slowly. Unlike most of the others, who shovelled theirs down as quickly as they possibly could, William liked to savour his every mouthful – at the end of a heavy day, when you're exhausted, even slops taste delicious, his thinking went. He sat alone, not interested in the grumbling, the cursing and crude conversations all around.

As soon as he'd finished, he headed back, darkness falling quickly.

"William." An urgent whisper made him stop abruptly. It was Mary.

"Over here!"

She was standing in the shadows, her hair falling loosely over her shoulders.

"Mary? It's getting dark. What are you doing here?"

"What do you think I'm doing here, you fool? I'm waiting to see you. So…" she placed her hands on her hips and leant forwards, "how was Cockle Creek? How were the…bricks?" She swayed a little and smiled, then brought her eyebrows closer together, bowing them into a mock-serious-looking frown.

"Fine Mary – yes, the bricks were fine, and…"

Mary tilted her head.

"And?"

"And, all the better for…for, the kiss…you did blow me a kiss, didn't you?"

"A kiss? Why would I blow *you* a kiss, William Parker?"

William looked at his feet.

"I'm sorry Mary, I –"

Suddenly, he felt the full force of her lips on his, her hands gripping his shoulders tightly, pulling him closer and closer, his world now slowly disappearing. The chill of his damp clothes, the raucous screams of convicts and their women, the neighing of horses and the shouting of orders were fading, just like the daylight. He felt his eyes start to sting, unaccustomed to tears of joy.

"Mary, please, don't ever let me go. I love you Mary Toft. I've just never had the words."

And once again, he felt his words stopped, felt her pressed close, where his body ended and hers started, no longer clear. He was merging, they were merging, lost in the anonymity of a dark Australian night.

"Oi! You two! Cut it out! Get to your rooms!"

A voice – the unmistakable voice of authority – shattered the intimacy of this, their first private moment.

"Get out of it, yer dirty dogs, before I chuck a bucket of water over you."

Almost before it had started, William and Mary were running their separate ways.

"I love you too," were the last words William heard as he ran; the last words he heard as he closed his eyes and fell asleep.

5

William sat in the shade of his hut, another long day at the brickfields behind him. He sat in silence, his head resting in his hands. It had been some weeks since he and Mary had kissed, and never before had he felt so confused; or more committed to the course of action upon which he had since set his heart. On a deep in-breath, he stood up, straightened his back, and pushed the hair away from his face. He would do as Matt had told him to do so many times – he *would* ask Mary to be his wife.

The walk to Mary's place was just a few minutes but to William was a lifetime. What if he had misread the signals that she seemed to be giving him? She was a kind girl who would not have failed to help anyone in distress, and she had no shortage of admirers, from the soldiers, like Sargent Smith, to the likes of ne'er-do-wells such as Tommy Gates. What if she said no, and recoiled from his advances? The camp was an unforgiving place where you could not avoid meeting, and every day would be an excruciating mix of deep shame and unbearable heartache, a public drama played out against a backdrop of knowing glances, sniggers and whispers. He arrived at her cottage, stopped, and listened, staying out of sight until he was sure it *was* her, quietly singing one of the many airs she sang to herself whilst working. His heart pounded madly and his mouth felt dry – he wanted to run away. Finally, unable to restrain himself any longer, he strode around the corner to find Mary tending something in her small garden – what, was of no importance to him as he took her into his arms and stopped her protestations with a kiss that was as long and deep as it was unexpected. When the embrace ended, Mary breathed in deeply, then laughing, took his face into her hands and kissed him again hard upon the lips. Both stood hugging, holding each other as if frightened by the thought that if they let go it would all prove to be a dream.

"William Parker, what took you so long?" he heard her ask, stroking his cheek, looking deep into his reddening eyes. "I thought I had done something to offend you."

William wiped away the tears that were starting to come, then took a small step backwards before dropping to one knee and taking her hands in his. The words came easily, without hesitation, and never had he felt so sure of anything in his life:

"Mary Toft. My beautiful, darling, Mary." He supressed a nerv-ous giggle. "Will you marry me?"

Mary looked down at where he knelt and hesitated, momentarily – the longest two seconds William had ever known – before answering.

"Yes. A million times, yes. Now get up, Will, and kiss me again."

William got to his feet, and lifted her off the ground. It was only then that he became aware, and heard the sound of clapping and the voices of Mary's fellow gardeners who had observed the proposal from beginning to end. Then he felt the hands shaking his, others ruffling his hair, followed by the babble of excited women, some of whom had hurried in from adjoining plots of land.

"Will you let *me* be your bridesmaid, Mary?"

"No Mary, *me*. I'm prettier than her."

"Away with you, you've both the look of donkeys!" said a third, "Come on Mary, choose *me*."

Mary and William pulled away from the small crowd that was starting to close in on them and ran, laughing, through the camp, back to the path leading to William's hut.

In a short time, they had left the excitement of their friends behind and slowed to a sauntering walk. Mary let her head rest on William's shoulder, their arms hooked at the elbow.

"Are you happy, Mary?"

"More than happy, Will; I don't think I have ever prayed so hard for something to come true…and it did."

William smiled and kissed the top of her head.

"And *I* have never felt so scared in my life. Awaiting the judge's verdict was nothing compared with what I went through this afternoon. I…" His sentence remained unfinished, stopped abruptly by the unwelcomed appearance of someone they both knew.

"Aw, Mary – you look so happy! So, you've finally gone and done it!"

Tommy Gates was leaning on a post, grinning, a piece of grass clenched between his teeth.

"Mr and Mrs Parker, eh? What a beautiful end to a beautiful romance. What more can I say?" he said, sneering, and walked a few paces towards them.

"Go to Hell, Tommy. And take your good wishes with you," Mary said, looking him in the eye, "You're a nobody, and you know it."

Gates allowed himself a chuckle before turning to William.

"Letting your little lady do the talking, I see, Parker. You never were much of a fighter from what I hear."

William said nothing, but gripped Mary's arm a little tighter.

"Well, I'll be on my way. Not to Hell. I'll always be around to see *you* again, Mary," said Gates, tipped his hat to William then blew a kiss at Mary.

Mary grabbed William by the arm as he started to move towards Gates who was retreating into the shadows.

"He's not worth it Will. Please, don't let him spoil our moment."

William allowed Mary to steer him away and back along the path to his hut. They walked for a minute in silence. Then William spoke.

"What do you know of Tommy Gates, Mary? I can see why *he* would want you, of course; but was there ever anything between you, you know-"

"No, Will. Of course not! *You* should know that." Mary had fire in her eyes. "Tommy, or *Thomas* Gates, as he was once known, is the scum of the earth, one of the worst. He was at the Assizes when we were there. You didn't see him?"

William shook his head.

"And even if I had, I wouldn't have remembered him. I don't remember much really, apart from the uproar when the judge changed my sentence. Who is he, what did he do?"

"I never told you. Tommy's from a family of toffs. Up your way, Hertford or some such place, I think. He thought himself a lady's man – all airs and graces – but he would take advantage of any young girl who came to work in the house; you know, servants and the like. Nobody wanted to know, so he did what toffs do and got away with it, Scot free, for years."

"So, why is he here?"

"Well, he pushed his luck too far with the daughter of another toff – one of his father's associates – raped her and put her in the family way. But then, of course, someone listens to *her* – she wore satin and lace, and that makes all the difference, you know."

"I know," said William, "I know."

"So, he's a bastard, and deserves to rot in Hell."

"Let's hope he does," said William, then opened the door of his hut so that they could finish what they had started earlier.

Early next morning, William and the future Mrs Parker lay together in silence. At this hour, even the birds and the creatures of the night were quiet, and neither wanted to break the spell that seemed to have enveloped them. Mary raised herself on an elbow and looked into his face, the first light of day playing across his features.

"Do you love me, Will?" she whispered, and traced the contours of his mouth.

William half opened an eye and smiled.

"Is the king of England rich?" he replied, sleepily, and pulled her down towards him, feeling the warmth and weight of her body against his. She rolled over, straddling him, then pulled herself away to look at him again, full in the face.

"And will your love last forever, Will? For richer, for poorer, in sickness and in health?" She counted on her fingers.

"Aye, and longer still, Mary. Till this forest is no more, till every tree and every leaf has gone, to build His Majesty's Ships."

"That, William Parker, is the correct answer," she said, and lowered herself gently into his arms.

6

The next day, and before the call for work, Mary and William stood side by side facing the Captain.

"So, Parker, you wish to take this woman, Mary Ann, to be your wife?"

"Yes, Sir, I do, and she has accepted my proposal," replied William, and stood a little straighter.

"And you, Mary Ann Toft. Do you love this man, William Parker? And do you agree to become his lawfully wedded wife?"

William turned to face her, anxiously awaiting her response.

"I do Sir. I love him with all my heart. In truth, I have done so for many months," Mary added, and looked across at William who smiled shyly, then looked at the Captain again.

The Captain said nothing for a few seconds and held both their stares.

"Very well," he said, simply, "Holy matrimony is a good thing – for the body and the soul. So, I will speak to the Reverend and we will arrange for it to be done without delay. This coming Saturday, half an hour before sunset." He scribbled something, paused, then met William's gaze with a look that was silent, but clear: *will that be all?* William thought his heart would stop, but managed to say a hurried thank you to the Captain before leading Mary outside.

Holding her tight, he gave her one last hug before they went their separate ways, he to the brickfields, she to the Tank Stream. And as they parted, he heard Mary calling his name and turned to see her blowing him a kiss, a kiss that seemed to drift effortlessly on the air across the hard ground between them.

★ ★ ★

Mary tried to stay still and calm as the others fussed around her. She had settled all arguments over bridesmaids by inviting the three of them to walk with her to the chapel, and now stood patiently as her closest friends worked feverishly to make her look as beautiful as possible for the ceremony to come.

"That William Parker, he won't recognise you by the time we've finished," said Daisy, as she smoothed down Mary's blouse, and straightened the creases in her dress so that they fell evenly to the ground.

"Well, I bloomin' well hope he *does*, Daisy! What would be the point of me turning up if just *anyone* will do?" Mary replied, keeping her head straight as Lorna, the second bridesmaid, brushed and re-brushed her hair.

"You know what them boys are like," said Daisy, pushing up her bosoms. The others fell about, laughing, until Lorna told them all off and reminded them that the time for the wedding was almost upon them.

"Are you excited? Or nervous? Or both, maybe?" Maggie, the youngest of the three, asked.

Mary tilted her head as if considering her answer, then declared simply that she was happy; just happy to have found love in the best man she had ever known.

"*And* you won't be a convict no more, Mary. He'll have made an honest woman of you, not like the rest of us prostitutes, as *they* likes to call us."

Mary bent forward and gave Daisy a hug.

"Married or not, Daisy, we aren't prostitutes, or whores, or tarts, or any of the other things they say we are. And anyway, your time will come. I mean, who could resist you lot with all your feminine charms?"

"Ooh! I don't know what you means," said Daisy, pouting, which set the four off laughing again.

When, at last, flowers had been woven into Mary's hair and a small bouquet placed in her hands, Lorna went inside and fetched a looking glass.

"Close your eyes…now open them again," she said.

Mary did as she was told, then focused on the image beyond the silvered surface – cracked and chipped as it was. The face she saw looking back at her was fragmented, and oddly distorted, but happy, and she spread her arms wide, drawing her friends together, thanking them again for all their efforts.

"Stop it, Mary, you'll set us all off," said Maggie. "Now then, who's going to stand where?"

On the other side of the camp, William sat talking to Matt. He held a short length of wire that he was carefully weaving into a make-shift ring, taking care to avoid any sharp ends that could hurt Mary's finger.

"How do I know it's going to fit, Matt?" he asked, squinting at the tiny loop between his fingers.

"It'll fit, Will, believe me. God will make sure of that. You do believe in The Almighty, don't you?"

"*Course* I do, Matt –"

"Well then, you can stop your worrying. If He can turn water into wine, making a ring to fit Mary will be no problem at all."

William laughed, handed the ring over to Matt, and made him promise not to lose it.

"Now, how do I look?"

"Your normal ugly self, Will," he said, pocketing the ring, "but I'm sure Mary won't turn you down. Now, go and wash yourself, or else you're going to be late for your own wedding – and she won't like that…"

★ ★ ★

Mary and the others turned the corner, and when they were in sight of the chapel slowed down and walked as sedately and demurely as they knew how. Mary caught the faint scent of her bouquet, and she smiled. Some convicts stood and watched, some shouted encouragement to the group, but most just got on with what they were doing. At the chapel, a small group of friends had already gathered, and at the front stood William and Matt, the best-man occasionally looking over his shoulder, keeping the groom abreast of developments. Dressed in clean black vestments, the Reverend Young was also waiting, a small bible cradled in his soft hands.

Mary sensed her breath shorten with every step, then felt the comforting arm of Daisy around her waist.

"One foot in front of the other, my girl. Every little step is one step closer to freedom."

Mary smiled again and lifted her chin.

The assembled friends parted allowing the bridal party to approach. Matt stepped aside as Mary came to stand next to William, who said nothing, but mouthed a silent hello.

The minister nodded a welcome and began his address to William, Mary and the congregation…

The service itself was a simple one, and William suddenly found himself saying "I do", placing the ring of wire on Mary's finger, and planting a kiss full upon her lips. The congregation cheered and clapped, and a shower of flower petals followed as the couple and their entourage turned and walked away from the chapel, one of their friends playing a reel on a fiddle that he had produced miraculously from somewhere beneath his jacket. They walked the short way to an area known as The Raceground, used by the convicts for gatherings and the few celebrations they were still allowed to enjoy; and in the distance, above the cove, the grand façade of the Governor's House looked down imperiously. Closer still was the site of the Old Gallows, both stark reminders of where, and who, they now were.

The newlyweds joined their fellow convicts who were enjoying themselves in the only way they knew how. The fiddler kept on playing, accompanied by a growing number of others who hearing the celebrations arrived late, blew at their whistles and banged their drums – the drinking had started before the chapel had faded from view. It was a happy scene that could have been transported from a verdant land on the far side of the world, a land that only a few years earlier had spat them out, like so much effluent.

After many hours of merriment, Mary stood before her new husband and slid her arms around his waist. "Looks like Matt and Daisy are getting on well," she said, nodding her head in the direction of their friends who were dancing and wheeling by the light of the fire. "Care to join them?"

"I don't think I could dance another step, Mrs Parker," he replied, as the events of the past two days started to take its toll.

"Oh, you *poor* old thing. Too much rum, Will," she teased him in the darkness, "let's sit you down so we can watch the youngsters dance."

William let himself be guided over to a rough bench that had been left empty, especially for the bride and groom. He watched with bleary eyes as his fellow convicts cavorted, silhouetted by the firelight, then felt Mary lean in against his side.

"Your mother should have been here, Mary; and your father. Should have given away his daughter. It's not right," he said sleepily.

He felt Mary squeezing his hand, kissing him on the cheek.

"An impossible dream, Will; and besides, my father would have drunk all the rum, leaving none for the rest of us."

"Sounds like a good idea to me, just now," said William, and closed his eyes, surrendering himself to the warmth of the fire, and to the music now wafting over him in waves.

As the flames began to gutter, Mary let the others know that she and William were leaving – going to William's hut, which would now become their home. The few still standing waved them on their way, wishing them well and shouting out bawdy remarks befitting the occasion. Daisy left Matt talking to friends, ran over and gave them both a final hug, reminding William to be a gentleman or he would have her to answer to.

William leant heavily on Mary as they headed for home, the sounds of the celebrations fading with the warmth and glow of the embers. Overhead, the stars winked at the pair and a bat flew across the moon in silent salute.

Then, when all was quiet, out of the darkness a face appeared; it held Mary's stare for a moment, spat, then disappeared into the night.

It was Tommy Gates.

7

It had been three months since the wedding. William and Matt had managed to find a quiet spot, a piece of land mostly cleared of bush but as yet not earmarked for anything in particular. Fifty yards away, groups of convicts stood and chatted, or pitch-and-tossed away what little wages they had amassed; the occasional Eora looked over then continued on their way; bored soldiers took no notice: it was the end of the working day.

"And?" said William, "What more do you know?"

Though he could not be heard, Matt looked around nervously.

"Not much Will, but enough to be worried on your behalf."

"So, you overheard a rumour – was it soldiers you say, or the Irish, or both? Who Matt?"

"A couple of soldiers. I was walking a few paces behind them. They'd had a drink, you know, not roaring drunk or anything, but enough to make them talk too loud, and they hadn't really noticed me, either."

"And they said...what exactly?" said William, probing.

"I couldn't hear every word, but I know it was something about a plan to bolt – and I heard them mention 'the Irish'."

William noticed a heron lift off effortlessly from a distant gumtree and head out towards the brickfields.

"Did they say anything about when they thought it was going to happen? The escape, I mean."

Matt shook his head.

"Nothing. But if it wasn't going to be sometime soon, why would they be talking about it now?"

"And did they mention any names? O'Connor, The Big Fellah, for example?"

"No, no names Will. But if the Irish are planning to bolt, you can bet your life that he's at the centre of things, and we know that the boys in red would just love to put him in his place. I don't want to worry you Will, but after what you told me, about your midnight meeting with him, I thought you needed to know."

"So now I know, what do I do about it, Matt?" William said anxiously.

"I don't know, Will," his friend responded, "I don't know. Just watch your back – yours *and* Mary's."

During the weeks that followed, wherever he was around the camp, William found himself eavesdropping on conversations, and listening hard...to a group of soldiers sitting together, sharing a pipe, thinking their chat was inaudible and of little interest to those nearby; to a gaggle of women at the Tank Stream, most of their talk around men of interest interspersed by howls of coarse laughter; to old lags, heads held close, filling the minutes at the end of the day; but mostly to the Irish, speaking in their whispers, jealously guarding their secrets beneath the veil of their strange and indecipherable language. But some words were impossible to hide: *O'Connor*, *bolt*, and *bush* amongst them. And then all would go quiet again until the next time when the same three words would prick his ears and make his heart beat faster.

"You're looking tired, my friend. End of a long day? Or Mary wearing you out, is she?"

William summoned up a smile, kicked out at a pebble, but carried on walking slowly.

"I am, Matt, but not for the reason you suggest. This O'Connor thing," he said, "it's worrying Mary so much she can't sleep, and it's starting that even I can't think of much else –"

Matt raised his hand, stopping him mid-sentence. A pair of soldiers passed by, barely giving them a glance.

"What have you heard Matt?"

"Same as you – the odd bits of tittle-tattle, things Daisy has heard at the stream –"

"Like what?" It was William's turn to interrupt.

"As I said, not much Will. And keep your voice down – you might attract the wrong sort of attention. So, she said she heard some hussy or other, Irish she was, gabbing off to one of her English friends. Daisy couldn't be sure, 'cos she'd gone quiet. but she thought she heard her whispering that some of the men were planning to make a break for it…and she thought she heard the name O'Connor too."

William clasped his hands together, his knuckles turning white. Matt averted his eyes. "Matt, when was this? Yesterday? Last week? When?"

"Ten days, maybe a fortnight ago? Whenever it was, nothing has happened, so perhaps it's all just gossip. You know how it is in this place, things get said, everyone gets excited, then nothing happens and it all dies down again. They like something to talk about, don't they? – a bit of scandal, something to take their mind off this place."

William nodded. "Yes, yes, you're right Matt; and if they haven't bolted by now, well, O'Connor has probably got cold feet and decided to stick it out, just like the rest of us!"

Matt smiled and gave William a friendly punch in the arm.

"That's the spirit, Will. Now, go home to your beautiful new wife and enjoy married life while you can. Me? I'm off to my own sad place, no feminine touches there…though I might try and see Daisy later!"

William straightened his shoulders, returned the punch, then wandered off to reassure Mary.

William, breathing hard and still shaking, brought his fists to his sides as ordered. His face was bruised and cut, his hair and shirt dripping wet.

"Sir!" he managed to say before wiping his mouth, turning his sleeve crimson.

"You look a bloody mess Parker," said the Captain, looking down his nose. "What happened this time?"

"He was involved –"

"Let Parker speak for himself, Private. I know he's not a man of many words but I think he's quite capable of answering for himself."

"Understood Sir. Beggin' your pardon."

The Captain nodded towards William. "Carry on, Parker."

"It was the Irish, Sir. Two of them jumped me by the water trough. Said they would kill me next time they had a chance. For what happened to O'Connor and to the ones who died."

"Indeed. And who was it who attacked you, Parker? Give me their names."

"Didn't see their faces, Sir. They jumped me from behind and held my head under the water so as I couldn't breathe. Couldn't do anything. I thought I was going to drown."

He spluttered and wiped more blood onto his arm, then cleared his eyes of the water still dripping from his hair.

"Any clues, Private?" The Captain turned to the soldier, who shook his head and gave a quiet laugh.

"No. No witnesses, Sir. And yer Irish will never split on each other. Thick as thieves that bunch."

"So. No witnesses. No names. And none of the Irish likely to land their fellow countrymen in it. And what *had* you done, Parker, to bring this upon yourself? Remind me."

William bowed his head, his eyes searching the floorboards for the best answer he should give.

"Parker?"

"They…they say that I gave O'Connor false information about what was out there. What I saw when I escaped –"

"When you *tried* to escape," interrupted the Captain.

"…when I *tried* to escape," William corrected himself.

"And did you? Give O'Connor *false* information? And for what reason?"

"*No* Sir. I just told him what I remembered about the bush to the west – the lay of the land, the trees and the dry riverbeds. I just told him the truth, and that there *was* no road to China. And I told him I didn't think anyone would make it out from here alive, and I warned him not to try it."

"Private. What's O'Connor's story – since he was caught and flogged?"

"Gone very quiet, Sir. He was a mess when we found him, when we brought him back. And after the flogging…well, he barely made it. But he lets his lackeys do his dirty work – and he's a fighter, Sir, and getting stronger by the day."

The Captain turned to William again.

"So, explain to me – why didn't you tell anyone about the plan? O'Connor's plan I mean. Why didn't you inform on them? You could have told any of the soldiers or even me. We could have nipped it in the bud. O'Connor would have had his flogging and the others would have been spared their untimely deaths. So, what stopped you?"

"Sir, with respect, you have no idea of what it is like to be a prisoner here, and this isn't the first time they have threatened me or my Mary."

"Threatened? What form did this take, and when?"

William took a deep breath.

"Where do I start, Sir? It's all the time. It's everywhere. It's the push in the back, the spitting, the whispers and dark looks, the nods and the winks, the words they use to Mary. It was always going to come to this. *I* can take it Sir, but Mary…"

The Captain got up from his seat and poured himself a brandy, swilling the rich brown liquid rhythmically around the glass. He paced his office slowly, deep in thought. Neither William, nor the soldier, said or did anything.

"Why should I *care*, Parker?" The Captain had stopped, and was standing close – so close William could smell the sweet bouquet of the drink. He stared ahead, mutely.

"Well, Parker? Why *should* I care?"

William stepped backwards before replying.

"I'd like a transfer, Sir."

"A transfer? You haven't answered my *question*, Parker."

"Answer the Captain, Parker!" the soldier blurted out before a look told him all that he needed to be told.

William stared straight ahead; the Captain's question unanswered. Why *should* he care?

"I don't know Sir. I don't know why you should care."

"In that case Parker, you may go."

The Captain waited until he and the soldier were alone.

"Private, we need to preserve the peace, especially between our Irish friends and the rest of them. From now on, I want you to make sure that Parker is assigned duties which keep him away from O'Connor and his men. Tell whoever needs to know. The same goes for his wife who is on no account to be left alone with any of O'Connor's friends – men or women. Do I make myself clear?"

"Yes, Sir. Orders understood. Parker and his missus to be kept clear of the Irish. I will make the arrangements, immediately, Sir!"

Christmas came and went, and plumes of smoke from bushfires were spotted rising from the distant Blue Mountains apart from which little of note happened, but were months which William and Mary would always remember as being some of the happiest times they would spend together. For the most part, Mary was content washing the colony's laundry, whilst William was happy to wallow in the mud of the brickfields knowing all the while that he was adding to Mary's workload. Their work was steady, but undemanding. Mary placed a bowl in front of William and joined him at the table.

"The scar's fading – almost gone, Will. You're nearly back to your handsome self."

"Nearly?" William smiled.

"Nearly," Mary replied, and brushed the hair away from his forehead. "But you know I like my men rugged," she added, before breaking into laughter.

William changed the subject.

"Any trouble with the Irish girls?" he asked.

"Not a thing. The odd glance across the stream, but nothing out of the usual. None of us was raised in a nunnery, so there's always language flying back and forth, but that's what it's like amongst us women. It would make you blush, Will, so it's best you just don't know."

William laughed and took another swig of beer.

"And what about you, Will? You haven't mentioned anything."

He allowed a mouthful of food to go down and shook his head. "Nothing. Whatever the Captain said after I saw him must have worked. Like with you, there's always a bit of banter, and a few of O'Connor's crew have thrown me some dirty looks, but what is anyone supposed to do? A cat can look at a king, and all that."

"Or a queen."

William looked confused. "Or a queen," he agreed, then reached across and took her left hand in his. "It seems like years ago, now."

"The wedding?"

"Yes, the wedding. The best day of my life."

"And mine," Mary said, squeezing his hand.

"Mary?" he said, allowing the word to linger, "do you ever think that your parents might know we are married?"

"My parents? How would they know we were married?"

"No, I realise that that would be impossible, but do you ever get the feeling they might?"

Mary thought for a moment before answering.

"No, Will, I don't. How could they?"

"But would they be happy, do you think?"

"Happy? I don't know. My dad would probably be glad to be rid of me; and my mother...well, I'm not sure."

"She wouldn't be happy?"

"No, I think she would be, but Will, we were never close. I think she loved me, but..." her voice trailed off. "But why do you ask?"

William shrugged. "I don't know. I just feel that they *should* know. It's too important for them *not* to know."

"Maybe you're right, Will," Mary nodded, "maybe you're right."

The light was fading as they finished their meal and cleared away the few utensils they possessed.

"And do you think there might be another wedding soon?"

"Whose?"

"Who do you think, Will? Matt and Daisy, obviously! They were kissing and hugging almost as much as we were. Don't you ever talk of such things?"

Again, William looked confused.

"No, not really. Do you and Daisy?"

"Haven't seen her much, to be honest," Mary said wistfully, "but if I *had* seen her, I'm sure that's what we would have talked about."

"Matt and Daisy, eh? I'm already looking forward to it."

Later, as they lay in bed, Mary continued to speculate on who might get married to whom, and William on whether Matt would make him his best man...

8

It was late in the day when Mary made her way to a part of the creek where the women were sometimes allowed to do the washing. She staggered a little under the weight of the bundle of clothes she carried and took care not to stumble and fall onto the hard earth of the forest path. Old tree stumps and thick roots competed with a tangle of creepers and tendrils to see which would be the first to bring her to her knees.

It was a ten-minute walk, and Mary passed groups of other women making their way back to camp, their damp bales steaming in the cool of the early evening. Some chatted noisily, but most walked home quietly, pressed down by the burden they carried; exhausted by life.

When she arrived, the muddy bank was deserted, and the only sounds she heard were the coarse laughs of the women disappearing into the forest depths and the cries of birds somewhere in the treetops. She stopped, rolled the clothes onto a small jetty, then splashed a little of the water onto her face. The coolness was good, and she closed her eyes, allowing herself a few moments before starting. Through the veil of her eyelids, she watched dancing shapes, points of red, white and yellow, dart from right to left, from top to bottom, in a display designed to entertain and lift her mood. Watching the performance, she smiled to herself, then suddenly stopped. A sound, immediately behind, made her hold her breath and, as she made to turn, to see who, or what, was near, a hand jerked her violently upwards, gripping her throat, threatening to squeeze the very life from her. Forcing her eyes to open wide, she saw nothing save the grey-blue of the sky and the blinding orange of the sun as it burst, like a gun, through the trees; her attacker breathed into her ear:

"Mary, Mary, quite contrary…" His warm breath was on her

neck, and as she turned to confront him a hand grabbed roughly at her breast.

"Mary. Just relax, and you won't get hurt."

Her face began to burn, her eyes to bulge, and the veins at her temple were ready to burst. With her head starting to swim, and when she sensed she must surely faint, the hand at her throat loosened a touch and she was at last able to gulp down her first breath in what felt like a lifetime. She coughed and bent double, unable even to strike out at her assailant, then looked up to see the figure of Tommy Gates standing over her.

"Aw, come on Mary, you know you've always wanted me," he wheedled, before pulling her towards him. His mouth pressed against her, searching for hers, his hands exploring the contours of her body beneath her thin clothing, tearing the blouse from her shoulders.

Summoning all her remaining strength she pushed him hard and spat full into his face, then let out a scream that sent the bright birds of the forest scattering noisily upwards, away to the sanctuary of the canopy.

"You bast—"

Gates's hand closed over her mouth, stopping her words, but not the well of fury from which she drew a strength she did not know she possessed. She bit down, hard, drawing blood from the fingers that now forced themselves between her lips. Then he too screamed, and she reeled at the sting of a vicious slap that knocked her sideward, into the shallow waters of the creek. As Gates fell to his knees, joining her in the water, she fought the pressure of his legs straddling hers, threatening to finish her off.

"You whore! Nobody refuses Tommy. I take what I want, Mary, and all I've ever wanted is you."

He started to loosen his belt as Mary, her hands slipping uselessly on the bed of the muddy shallows, struggled to wriggle free. He was muttering incoherently to himself, cursing the buckle, fidgeting with his belt – his attention momentarily distracted…and then it was his turn to choke, as a canal-digger's forearm tightened around his throat like a vice.

And in that instant, Mary saw all thoughts of her and her feminine charms evaporate from his face into the warm air, like the light steam rising from the washer-women's bundles. She heard him grunt, watched him adjust his footing, then push up hard, the back of his head smashing into William's jaw with a thud. William cried out loudly, then Gates span round and grabbed William blindly by the arm, pulling them both into the mud with a splash. Seizing her chance to escape, Mary pulled herself free of Gates' legs and heaved herself onto the jetty side, then looked round desperately for anything she could use as a weapon, to join William in the fray.

As both men struggled to stand, William's eyes re-focused just in time to see the flash of a blade plunging down towards his face. An instinctive movement found him grasping, then wrenching the knife from Gates's grip, blood and the sharp stab of pain taking several more seconds to arrive. He heard Mary's cries echo through the forest, wiped the filth from his eyes, then charged – his head crashing into Gates' stomach. Forcing him backwards across the mud, William fell on him, pinning him down as Gates had pinned down Mary earlier. With his strength almost spent, William threw himself forwards one last time, forcing Gates's face down into the murkiness of the water. The water now ran blood-red, the surface an explosion of bubbles from Gates's nose and mouth which quietened only when his lungs finally emptied.

"William!"

Mary's voice was the last thing he heard before the musket butt turned his world from day into night and he slumped forward to join Gates in the shallows. Then all was silent, save the noise of the birds in the trees.

Mary sobbed as she watched the soldier drag Gates sideways, grabbing him by the collar to heave him to the safety of the shore. Immediately, she threw herself upon William and cradled his head in her lap, shielding the bareness of her bosom from the knowing eyes of Sergeant Smith.

His head throbbed badly and his palm was on fire. William stood bowed, with his hands bound behind his back, waiting for the arrival of the Captain.

"Straighten up lad! You're not on bloody 'oliday!" Sergeant Smith poked him in the back hard, adding another bruise to his already battered body. William said nothing, but stood a little more upright, when the door of the office opened suddenly and the Captain strode in.

He stopped, looked at William briefly, then sat at his desk. He lent back, all the time watching William intently. William continued to stare at the floor.

"What is it with you and water, Parker? You're like oil. You just don't mix. First, if my memory serves me well, it was your boss's son who perished, and now, it's one of your convict friends –"

"Not a friend, Sir. *Not* a friend."

Another poke in the back jerked William forwards, an unspoken order to shut up, to speak only when given permission.

"*As* I was saying, Parker…one of your convict friends, you almost drowned him too. Fortunately for you, Sergeant Smith here was around to save Gates, and then you, *deus ex machina*, from landing yourself on another murder charge. The journey this time, Parker, would have been considerably shorter than the one that brought you to Botany Bay – the final six feet, you'd have been dangling at the end of a rope." He flattened a sheet of paper onto his desk and picked up a quill. "What shall I write, Parker?" he asked with genuine bemusement. "A hundred, two hundred lashes? Solitary confinement? Norfolk Island? All three?" He leant back in the chair and laid the quill on the desktop.

William raised his head to look directly into the other man's eyes.

"Sir, for my own fate I now hardly care, but for my Mary's sake I *beg of you* to allow us a transfer, away from Gates, away from others who would do us harm. Anywhere but here. You have children, Sir, a daughter, I believe, of a similar age to Mary. Would you stand back and watch her ravaged by –"

The soldier broke in, but was waved aside by the Captain.

"Let the prisoner continue, Smith. I am man enough to hear his words, unrefined as they may be. Now, Parker, carry on."

"Tommy Gates had followed Mary to the creek, Sir. He intended to...rape her, Sir. If I had not seen him disappearing into the forest and, suspecting the worst, followed him, he would have finished what he had already started. Or worse, Sir. He could have killed her!"

The Captain raised his hand then looked across at the soldier.

"Sergeant Smith. Describe for me what you saw when you arrived at the creek."

Smith stepped forward and coughed.

"One of Parker's friends – Matthew Hodges – had seen Gates run into the bush and then spotted Parker 'ere following him. They'd both left their work stations, gone off without permission. Knowing the bad feeling between them he'd come running across to me and told me what he'd seen, so I decided to follow them, to see what they was up to. I didn't know nothing about Parker's missus as most of the women were on their way back to camp carrying their washing, and I didn't think anything of it. When I arrived at the creek, Mary Parker was on the jetty, soaking wet and crying. And I could see from her torn top that she had, beggin' your pardon Sir, been 'assaulted'. The two men were in the shallows just nearby with Parker kneeling on Gates's chest, I think it was, pushing his 'ead under the water. There was blood everywhere and Parker was screaming like he was mad. So, I came up behind him and gave him a good un on the back of his head with my musket 'ere, then dragged Gates to the side where he lay till he started spluttering and coughing his guts up –"

"Yes, thank you Smith, enough. I think I get the picture. And what of Parker and his wife?"

"She, Mrs Parker, joined him in the water and held his 'ead, like this Sir, sort of cradling him till he came round too. Then after a bit, when they'd both come round like, I marched them back to camp and put both the men under lock and key. She went back to her cottage, I think, and got herself some dry clothing. And that's about it, Sir, until this morning."

"And Gates?"

"Still in the lock-up, Sir. Hardly the worse for wear."

The Captain leafed again through a sheaf of papers on the desk, stopping occasionally, and writing something that William could neither see properly nor read.

"Take the prisoner outside, Smith, I need a little time to think. I'll call you when I'm ready."

William was led onto the veranda, and forced to stand while Smith sat on a bench leaning forward onto his musket. Outside, life went on as normal and few bothered to look up at the forlorn figure in leg-irons or the bored-looking soldier yawning in the heat. It was business as usual, just another day in the life of the colony. After a few minutes, Smith broke the silence, remarking that the Captain seemed to be taking a long time over his deliberations.

"Could be a good sign, but could be bad. He's had a lot on his plate just recently, what with the drought, them useless boatmen losing the grain up at Hawkesbury, and the bleedin' Irish runnin' riot here, there and everywhere…"

Smith shook his head, and looked across at William, but he wasn't listening – he was breathing in deeply, steadying himself on the wooden rail. The thought of another flogging had turned his bowels to water, while the idea that he and Mary might be forced apart was enough to break his heart. His mind wandered back to the precious moments of happiness that he and Mary had had since she had become Mrs Parker: the first time they had legitimately shared the same hut, the same bed…

"Sergeant Smith. Bring in the prisoner!" The sound of the Captain's voice jolted William from his daydream, returning him to the harsh reality of the moment.

"After you," said Smith with an ironic flourish, then whispered "and remember to stand up straight," before he allowed William to shuffle ahead of him, back into the shade of the office.

"Stand up straight!" Smith barked, "and look at the Captain!"

Faulks gave Smith a weary look before standing to face William who did as he was told and faced the older man.

"It's not been easy, Parker," he said, straightening his jacket, "but I *have* reached a decision."

William bowed his head, fearing the worst.

"Tommy Gates, in spite of his good birth, is a recalcitrant of the worst order who, despite our efforts, has proved himself, a man of unredeemably low morals."

William raised his head a little.

"So, after much thought, I have decided that in this case you were not to blame. You did what any good husband would have done, particularly in the afterglow of your wedding, and Gates got what he deserved. You may thank Sergeant Smith here for saving you from yourself." He gestured towards the soldier and William nodded his acknowledgement.

"Thank you, Sarge."

The Captain pushed back his shoulders before continuing.

"I have decided, therefore, that Gates, and Gates alone, shall receive the lash. In his case, the hundred he deserves and is no doubt expecting, while you, Parker, shall be allowed to go free. But," he levelled a look at William, "I do not consider it necessary to move you. Gates will learn his lesson the hard way and will leave you well alone."

William was about to respond when Faulks nodded to Smith and he suddenly found himself in the sunshine once again.

"Bit close for comfort, Parker, but Gates has had it comin' for months. The Captain is a fair man, but doles it out when it's needed – as you know already, son."

William nodded, too stunned to say anything.

"Right, get back to that wife of yours, and I'll see you bright and early in the mornin'."

"Thanks, Sarge," was all William could muster before rushing home to Mary with the news.

9

The day of Gates's flogging followed swiftly. That evening William and Mary sat facing each other across a simple table, one that William had made with his own hands. The light was disappearing fast and they spoke by the glow of a candle.

"How do you feel?" Mary asked.

"Don't know," William replied. "Numb, I think. Glad it's over, I suppose, but no joy at what happened. And you, Mary," he said, reaching across and cupping her hands in his, "what about you?"

She shook her head and shrugged.

"Don't know either. I'm pleased he got his punishment and I'm relieved he won't be around for a while, and," she paused, "and I know it's unchristian, but I don't feel sorry for him. Do *you* Will?"

William took back his hands.

"I hate what he did, but I couldn't watch more than the first two lashes. It's inhuman, what they do to us. I felt the blows myself; my back stung with each crack."

"What if he'd succeeded, Will? You know, if you hadn't stopped him and he'd raped me, like he did the girls in England. What then? What would you have felt, then?"

William stood up quickly and walked to the window, staring out into the dark night sky.

"I don't know, Mary, I don't know. Maybe I would have killed him myself."

For the next few weeks, life at the colony rolled on and Gates was in no fit state to cause trouble. Even O'Connor was nowhere to be seen, and his compatriots too seemed to be keeping their distance. For his part, William was happy to keep his head down, to believe that his dealings with The Big Fellah were a figment of his imagination, and to think only of his new life with Mary. Around the camp, there was little out of the ordinary to report. The everyday occurrences of beatings, rape, and deaths went almost unnoticed, but then the "everyday" of life as a convict was not the everyday of most people in the world beyond the confines of New South Wales.

It was a Sunday evening, the end of the colony's day of rest. William was sitting, staring into space, the workings of a door lock, a screwdriver, and an oily rag spread out before him. His hand lay unmoving on a rusty bolt.

"A penny for them, Will?"

Mary laid a trug full of garden vegetables on the table.

"Oh…daydreaming – thinking about my father, actually. I always think about my father when I'm fixing things."

Mary came and stood next to him, her arm around his shoulders.

"We had a bolt, on the door in our cottage – the one before we moved into the lock-keeper's house –" he continued, "and it was always sticking. My pa would take it off to try to get it to work, put it back, then a week later have to take it off again; it would always end up sticking, but he would never give up trying to fix it. He was always doing something around the house, especially on the roof, which used to leak whenever it rained – which was always. But he never complained, just got on with it. I think he saw it as protecting his family."

"Do you miss him, Will?"

"Of course. Don't you miss *your* father?"

William felt Mary stiffen.

"I haven't told you everything about him, Will." She turned to look out of the window and stood fidgeting with a piece of thread come loose from her blouse. "He was a drunkard, and when he was in his cups, he was one you would best avoid. We'd hide beneath the blankets and pretend we were not there, then stay hidden until we heard him snoring, before poking our heads out. But he was just like all the other men where we lived – that's what London's like."

"Did he…*hurt* you, Mary?" William asked.

"No, not really. And nothing like that Will. We all got a clip, but it was Ma who copped it worse. Whatever she did, it was never enough."

Mary paused and let out a long sigh.

"So, no. I don't miss him, though I suppose I did love him in a way."

William pulled Mary down so she was sitting on his knee, her head leaning into his shoulder.

"Well, *I* love you Mary," he said, and gave her a gentle squeeze.

She said nothing in reply, but noting his grazed knuckles dabbed away a smear of blood with her thumb.

"And I you; and your hands, Will. Are they your father's hands?"

"He had – has – strong hands. A canal-digger's hands. But he was – *is*," William corrected himself again, "a kind man. Never raised his hands to any of us. They were good parents to us children." He pushed the hair away from Mary's face.

"Do you think we would make good parents, Will?" she asked looking into his eyes?

William took her face into his and kissed her, long and deep.

"Well, only if we had a child," he answered, and with a smile carried her to the bedroom.

"Will, it's Monday. You need to get up."

William groaned and lent over her, his head propped up on his elbow. He smiled.

"*Stop* it Will. Be gone!" she giggled, "If you're late for roll-call you'll get it in the neck; give *me* a bad name."

William rolled out of bed and pulled on his breeches.

"It's all right for *you*, Mary, with your later start. It's another day covered in shit for me –"

"*Language*, Mr Parker," Mary mocked, as William went outside to find himself some breakfast.

William joined the others, as usual standing in line ready for their day's work. Names were called, ensuring that no one had absconded, escaped into the night, and on this occasion, nobody had.

"Parker."

"Here Sir!"

"Fall out. The Captain wants to see you."

"Me?"

William felt his throat tighten, his pulse begin to race.

"What for Sir? I haven't done anything."

"I don't bleedin' know. Just get yourself over to his hut. *Now*, Parker!"

A short time later, William arrived at the door of the Captain's hut. He straightened and knocked once.

"Come."

William entered and took off his hat, twisting it in his hands.

"Ah, Parker. Come in. How are you this morning?"

For a moment, William was unable to speak. The Captain had never asked him such a question before.

"Well. Thank you, Sir. And yourself?"

"Fine. Thank you," he replied and picked up a sheet of paper from his desk.

"The last time we spoke, some several weeks ago, you had been involved in an altercation with Tommy Gates. Am I right?"

"Yes, Sir," William replied slowly.

"Have you had any more trouble from him or his cronies?"

William felt confused, unsure where this was going.

"No, Sir. They've left us well alone."

"Good, good," the Captain replied, nodding, continuing to study the paper. Then he looked up.

"Very well, Parker, I'll explain. You have heard of Mr Campbell?"

"Of Campbell's Wharf? Of course, Sir. He's famous. Everybody's heard of him."

"Well, and you may not know of this, Mr Campbell's foreman, a man of some experience, was killed last week. The unfortunate fellow was crushed by one of his own bullock carts, loading, or unloading, I don't know which, down at the quayside. A complete accident, but these things happen, I suppose. But one man's misfortune may present another with an opportunity, and Mr Campbell himself has asked if I know of any prisoner who may, so to speak, fill the dead man's shoes. And I thought of you."

William held his tongue, a thousand thoughts swirling through his head.

"Have you nothing to say, Parker?" the Captain ventured shortly.

"Yes, Sir. Sorry, Sir." William gathered his thoughts, then spoke slowly and deliberately. "I'd be most honoured, Sir, to accept the position, if it is, indeed, being offered to me. And what of Mary, my wife?" he added, emboldened.

"Mrs Parker? She will work for Mrs Campbell – as a domestic. Help her to run the household and so on. And – importantly for you both I suspect – you will be rehoused on Pitt Street in the centre of town, some distance from the camp. The unfortunate deceased has no further use for the premises and he had no wife, so, as I said, one man's misfortune –"

"Yes, Sir, I'd be happy to accept Mr Campbell's kind offer," William interrupted; unable, despite the circumstances of the other's demise, to restrain the grin that was spreading across his face.

"Very well. You will report at the wharf tomorrow at seven – the brickfields know not to expect you – and move into your new accommodation the day after. Mrs Parker should go to the Camp-bells' house at noon so that she can be similarly briefed on her new role. Do I make myself clear?"

William stood to attention and grinned further.

"Yes, Sir, very clear. And thank you, Sir," he said, before closing the door and running to share the good news with Mary.

10

It was his first day at the wharf. William had got up early and Mary had made sure that he looked like a foreman Mr Campbell would be proud of. She had smoothed back his hair and straightened his jerkin. *You'll be fine*, she'd said, as she patted away a small stain with a finger. And now, he stood outside the warehouse, mouth dry, a strange feeling in his stomach, waiting for the others to arrive. The air was clear and cold, a light breeze blowing in from the still waters of the cove, and all around him, the wharf was starting to wake up. Gangs of men were heading here and there under the lazy eyes of bored-looking soldiers: a solitary figure approached him – very tall, and stocky, silhouetted by the rising sun. William put his hand to his eyes, straining to see.

"You must be the new boss," a voice said, flat and unwelcoming.

William stepped to the side, allowing him to see the face – it was angular and lean, the head close-shaved. He stretched out his hand, and it remained unshaken.

"I'm Parker," he said, "William Parker. I've come to replace your old foreman, Mr...I'm afraid I don't know his name."

"Smith. John Smith. Life crushed out of him." A finger pointed to the cobbles. "Just over there."

William nodded. "I'm sorry. A terrible way to go."

The other man, no older than himself, stood sullenly, waiting for William to continue.

"And you are?" William asked.

"Smith. John Smith," he replied, then, noting the look of puzzlement on William's face, added, "He was my father."

William immediately lost his smile and looked at the ground.

"I'm sorry. I –"

"No need. He was a bastard. Treated his men like he treated his beasts. If the bullocks hadn't got him, one of us would've," Smith added, then turned as two more men approached from the direction of The Rocks.

"Are these men part of our gang?" William asked, welcoming the distraction.

"Yes, Sir," – the word seemed to stick in his throat – "White and Mulligan."

"And you can drop the Sir, Smith; Mr Parker will do just fine," said William.

Smith nodded, but said nothing in return.

The other men made their way over.

"Gentlemen," William said, to which the pair nodded their good-mornings.

"My name's William Parker. And you must be Messrs White and Mulligan, I believe."

White, as short and wiry as Mulligan was tall and stout, offered his hand.

"Good day to you, Mr Parker. Aye, I'm Mackenzie White – Mac. I take it you're the new foreman," he said.

"I am indeed, Mr White. And you," William continued, turning to the other man, "must be Mulligan."

"You've got me in one. Michael Mulligan – at your service, Sir," he said with an ironic bow.

William looked around him, unaccustomed and uncomfortable in this new position of authority, and, spotting a small group of soldiers sauntering towards them, turned to Mac.

"So, how are the members of the Corps towards you?"

"That lot? Nae too bad, as long as you behave. Bunch of laddies in the main. Would rather be elsewhere, just like the rest of us, if you follow my meaning."

"I do. And do they supervise you during the day – doing your daily work?"

Mac shrugged, "What would you say Mick? Out for an easy life?"

"Aye, an easy life is how I would describe it. Keep themselves to themselves. Except, that is when there's a delivery of rum. Then they suddenly come alive, like rats scurrying the length and breadth of the quay. Beady eyes all over you, makin' sure the same number of barrels that come in make it to the warehouse shelves."

Mac laughed; Smith stared into the distance.

"*And,*" Mulligan continued, getting into his stride, "when the gaffer, Mr Campbell, makes a visit. When he's around, then they're all for marchin' and shoutin', making themselves look all official an' that. And when he's gone, it's back to the card games and takin' a nap while they can."

William grinned.

"And Mr Campbell? Is he a fair man?" He looked back at Mac.

"He's from the Borders – like me – so, aye, he's fair, and favours the little man, but he's nae one to be messed with all the same. In fact," he said, gesturing to a tall gentleman striding towards them, "you can see for yoursel'. That's him coming down the road."

William pulled back his shoulders and stood straighter as his new boss approached.

"Mac, Mulligan, Smith," he said, greeting each with a small nod, "and Mr Parker, I presume."

William stepped forward and took the hand that was offered.

"Yes Sir, Mr Campbell, I'm very pleased to meet you."

"And me, you," he replied. "Smith and Mulligan, you can get off to work. Mac, you and Mr Parker here can come with me. Come into my office."

William and Mac followed Campbell into the warehouse and then into a modest, well-ordered backroom.

"Please, gentlemen, sit down," he said, in an accent that echoed that of Mackenzie White. "Welcome to Campbell & Company, Mr Parker; so, what do you know of what we do here at the wharf?"

William cleared his throat. "Well, I know that you run the most successful warehouse in Sydney, Mr Campbell; that you deal in livestock, grain, spirits, and now I believe, seal skins and oil." Encouraged by a nod and the hint of a smile, he continued, "And I think I heard that you have purchased grazing land, on the Canterbury estate, mainly for the cattle that you import."

"You heard right Mr Parker, and I'm pleased you have taken the trouble to find out a little about the company you will be working for. I have heard some good things about your ability to work with animals, and I hope you now show the same facility for working with men." He turned to his fellow countryman, "Mac, I want you to spend the day showing Mr Parker around the place. Show him the warehouses and introduce him to some of the men. And take him down to the quay. We've a shipment arriving this morning as *The Hindostan* has *finally* made it into harbour." He gave Mac an exasperated look and drummed his fingers. "Oh, and give him a tour of the stables, because," he said, turning to William, "as you know, you and the others will be spending much of your time with the oxen and horses. And, *you're* in charge of the gang. So now, unless you have any questions, I'll bid you good morning. We'll speak more at another time." And with that, he sought out his spectacles, carefully poring over a mass of figures in the ledger lying open on his crowded desk.

William and Mac returned from the stables and now sat on large sacks of maize, piles of which reached almost to the roof. The air was filled with dust and William had to fight off the urge to cough. Around them, groups of men dragged and carried, the clamour of their voices reverberating across the vast space of the warehouse before losing itself in the rafters high above their heads. It was the biggest building William had been in since leaving England.

"So, this is Mr Campbell's warehouse," Mac said gesturing, "well, one of several in fact. Mainly grain in this one. Others house whatever people choose to send us from overseas. Stuff comes in, stuff goes out. It's not complicated. As you've already seen, we leave the numbers to Mr Campbell. Spirits though, and I mean rum, gets special attention, particularly from the members of the Corps."

He looked at William to check he understood.

"In this place, rum is money y'ken, so it's locked away, and is under guard, day and night," he said, then cupped his hands to his mouth and shouted for silence. As soon as it was quiet, he stood up and turned to William, introducing him to the men as *the new*

John Smith. "Remember your manners, watch your language, and don't forget to say good-morning," he said, before telling them to get back to work. William heard grumbling and a few muttered *morning*s as Mac led him to the door. "Come on," Mac said as William strained to hear over the resurgent voices, "let's go down and see what's going on at the waterfront."

As they were walking William asked a question that had been running through his mind all morning.

"Mac, you obviously know the ropes and Mr Campbell seems to like you; why didn't he choose you for the foreman's job?"

"Oh, aye – I thought you might ask that. The truth is, I was not interested. I'm a good man to have in the room, as they say, but I'm getting on, and Mr Campbell needed someone with more energy than I could offer. So, he asked the Captain, and when he heard you were looking, he decided on you instead. Don't worry yoursel', there's no hard feelings, Mr Parker."

They did not have far to walk and soon they were standing looking over the waters, out towards the Heads of the harbour. *The Hindostan,* a three-master, just arrived from India, was being unloaded, and a babble of instructions, English mixing with a language that William neither understood nor recognised, formed the backdrop to a frenzy of activity. Dozens of dark-skinned sailors, many in white trousers and neat woollen caps, filled the wharf.

"Lascars," Mac explained, "hard-working, dependable, and *cheap* – less than sixpence a day. They'll work for whoever hires them and move between ships without complaining."

Elsewhere, men of all shapes and sizes, brown, white and yellow, made themselves busy, rolling and stacking barrels, humping sacks, arguing, cursing, wiping their brows; and in the distance William spotted the two men he had met earlier leading a team of oxen across the cobbled street, the wagon piled high with more grain for Mr Campbell's warehouses.

"Is that Smith and Mulligan I can see?"

"Aye, they know what to do, but need a firm hand sometimes," said Mac, looking to where William's gaze had settled. "They work hard enough, but are quick to get away once the task-work is over. 'Other things to do,' is what they say, you know, to bring in a bit of extra for themselves, and in Mick's case, his expanding brood of bairns."

"And Smith?" William asked.

"Aye, well, he keeps his cards close to his chest, so enough said, if you follow my meaning. Let's leave it at that."

Later, they joined Smith and Mulligan for their food break.

"Mac here show you the sights, did he? The palaces and boulevards that make up Campbell's Wharf," quipped Mulligan.

"He did indeed, Mick. The stables and the warehouse. I can see I have a lot to learn, and in a short time too."

Mulligan winked, and tore a strip off his lump of dry beef.

"And you, John," William asked, "what do you think about the work here?" Smith stared at the floor, his bare forearms resting on his knees.

"Me?" He shrugged as he looked up, "I fuckin' 'ate the place. Don't everybody?" he said, and went back to looking at his feet.

William allowed a few seconds to pass.

"Your hand, John; looks nasty. How did you hurt it?" He pointed to Smith's knuckles – bruised and bloodied.

Smith quickly withdrew his right hand, and William noted a swift exchange of glances between him and Mac before he answered. "Loading stuff, the other day. Barrel or something – bastard rolled and landed on me. I'm alright now," he added, kneading the damaged fist with his left hand.

"Glad to hear it," said William, and finished his own meal in silence.

Following a short meeting during which Campbell had told him some more about his company and what he expected of his men, William bade him goodnight and made his way back home.

An oil lamp relieved the gloom of the room where Mary was sitting, needle in hand, a small pile of shirts next to her. "Welcome home, boss. How was your first day in charge?"

William came over and kissed her, then made himself comfortable, sitting atop an old wooden chest.

"Good. I met Mr Campbell, who seemed to like me. Told me he welcomed some new blood. Then, I looked around the stables and the wharf and met my gang. Three men – Mac, who's a Scot, Mick from Dublin, and John Smith, from London, I think."

"And what did you think of it, and can you do the job? I'm sure you can, Will, but what do *you* think?"

William yawned, and stretched out his arms, his palms upturned.

"I didn't see anything that I couldn't do. Just got to learn to work with the ox teams but I think I'll have a good teacher in Mac."

"And the others? Did you take to them?" Mary pushed for more information.

"I did," said William, then thought a little more, "... apart from Smith. He's built like a barn. His father was the one who was killed – or so the story goes."

"Oh! The poor boy, Will-"

"No, Mary, but that's just it," William interrupted, "he wasn't upset about it. Called his father a bastard."

Mary placed the needle carefully down on the table and came over to join William on the chest.

"Well, maybe he's still in mourning. Grief does strange things to people." She patted his knee. "Come on, let's have something to eat..."

Later, as they lay in bed, Mary continued to quiz William about his day.

"Mary, enough about my day, with its stockmen, swearing and sweat. What about *your* first day at the grand house? What about Mrs Campbell and how she treated you?"

Mary sighed and rolled towards him.

"Upstairs and downstairs and in my lady's chamber."

William smiled, recalling the childhood rhyme.

"Will, after years of scrubbing and washing in the Tank Stream, *anything* would be better. Look, see my hands."

William strained to see in the half-light of a candle, and shook his head

"They're *white*, Will. Not red-raw and itching. I spent the day tidying and dusting, lifting nothing heavier than an emu feather. Mrs Campbell's clothes are clean, soft and colourful, her shoes shiny and without holes. It's another world, Will, but one I'm allowed to visit – for a few hours at least."

"I'm so pleased you have had a good start," said William, slurring his words, drowsy and beginning to fall asleep.

"This place is a hard place Will," Mary continued, speaking as much to herself and the darkness, as to William. "All cold: stone, wood, and metal. No softness. Even the people are hard; hard people living hard lives."

She stopped as William's heavy breathing told her he was asleep.

"Night, Will. I love you," she said, and kissed his cheek, before snuffing out the candle.

11

William and Matt walked the length of Pitt Street, leaving Mary and Daisy to themselves. It was Saturday night and the streets were teeming with people from all corners of the colony. The sound of raucous laughter permeated the air as convicts and soldiers mingled, questions of rank and position forgotten – for one night at least. A figure lay slumped in a doorway, and on the corner, a group of Eora men stood drinking, the bottle moving quickly between them as one, then the other, took a swig of cheap rum.

"Good to see you Will. It's been too many months."

"You too, mate," said William, then, grabbing Matt by the arm, pulled him through the door of The Red Cow.

The sound of fiddles and a tambourine, mixed with loud voices and the high-pitched laughter of women, drew them further inside.

The two men negotiated a long, dark corridor, brushing past a soldier and a convict woman, her skirts hitched round her waist, and found their way into the main room. The place was already crowded, with most of the customers standing around or leaning on the bar. William spotted a small table near the back wall and signalled to Matt to sit down opposite his friend.

"I'll get these," he said above the noise, and pushed his way through the dense crowd to the bar, choosing to ignore the grumbles of customers already in their cups. He slapped two coins on the counter, the barman handing him a pair of tankards in return; then, jostled from all sides, he got to the table and sat down.

"So, Will, you were going to tell me; about married life. Do you recommend it?"

William put down his drink and raised his eyes to the ceiling, for several seconds appearing to contemplate his answer.

Matt frowned. "Will?"

"*Absolutely*, Matt!" he beamed, "No doubt about it. You've just got to make sure you have chosen the right woman…and is Daisy the right woman?"

Matt returned the smile and tapped his nose. "Ah, that would be telling." He paused, then took another draught of beer. "And no little Parkers yet?"

"No, none as yet…but not for want of trying."

Matt grabbed his tankard and raised it again.

"*To trying*, Will."

"*To trying*," William replied, laughing.

Across the room, the argument over what music to play had come to an end, and the fiddles had started up again – a sad lament, this time, accompanied first by a handful, and then by a throng, of drunken Irish voices.

"And how is it in the camp, Matt? What news of Tommy Gates and friends?"

Matt shrugged.

"Nothing to report. He's kept his head down since the flogging. And as for his friends…well, does he have any? No. It's all been very quiet."

"Good to hear it." William leant in and kept his voice low, "and what of O'Connor? Any talk of the escape?"

Matt checked that no one nearby was listening before he replied.

"The Big Fellah? I haven't seen him since he was caught, so not much to report there either. Just the usual dark whisperings by this lot, if you know what I mean."

He looked over to where the fiddlers and singers were in full voice – arms around each other's shoulders, tears in their eyes – and banged his empty tankard on the table.

"So – another one, Will?"

"Well, Matt, why not?"

Several beers, and many ballads later, the music suddenly stopped and the bar began to empty, groups of men and women surging unsteadily towards the door at the back of the room.

"Will?" Matt looked at his friend, uncomprehending.

"It'll be a fight – in the yard. Fancy it?"

"Why not, Will? Think the Corps might try to stop it?"

"What? No; they probably *arranged* it Matt. Watch your pockets and keep your money to yourself."

Following the others, they made their way to the rear of the house. Rush-lamps and lanterns, supplementing the light of the full moon, illuminated an open space, cleared and ready for the contest. By now, the crowd had organised itself into a rough circle about thirty feet across, the area doubling up as a ring. As anticipation mounted, the noise was growing ever louder. William and Matt joined the others as they craned their necks to see who was going to emerge, stripped to the waist, ready to punch their opponent into oblivion. A lookout gave the all-clear and a burly man stepped into the ring, and using a length of wood scratched a line across its diameter. He raised his hands for quiet and eventually, amid much cursing and hushing, the noise subsided and he was able to make himself heard.

"Ladies *and* gentlemen!"

"Don't see no bleedin' ladies, here!" shouted a man.

"Don't see no bleedin' gentlemen, neither!" a woman replied, the laughter leading to a further long delay.

"Ladies and gentlemen," he tried again, "welcome to the Battle at the Red Cow. We have for you this evening two fighters, two *bulls* who I can guarantee, will not be *cowed* by this occasion!"

Some laughed, and a few groaned – most just shouted and told him to get on with it. William and Matt moved around the circle to get a better view.

The master of ceremonies continued unabashed, announcing that the first fighter was a favourite of the crowd, an Irish pugilist by the name of Patrick – *The Punch* – O'Sullivan.

A huge cheer went up as the wiry figure of the crowd's darling emerged from the shadows, fists already raised, his small eyes darting from left to right like a hunter searching for its quarry. Will looked at Matt and pulled a worried face. His friend responded with a lopsided grin and a disbelieving shake of the head.

"And," the announcer continued, "from Southwark – that's in fuckin' London, England – in case you don't know," he leered at the crowd, "we have our challenger: John – *The Slugger* – Smith!"

A loud boo rippled around the yard, then shouts of encouragement from the Londoner's small group of supporters. Smith appeared, taller and heavier than his opponent, and stood in the centre of the ring, punching the air and smirking at his detractors. All around, the voices – both Irish and English – grew louder and louder, and as the tension mounted, and the money started to exchange hands, scuffles broke out, people pushing and shoving to get a better look.

William turned to his friend. "Well, well, well. Talk of The Devil and he's sure to appear."

"Meaning?" said Matt.

"Remember the Smith I told you about earlier?" William nodded in the direction of the ring. "That's the very man. Explains his damaged hand, doesn't it? I knew he was a ne'er-do-well, and I was right."

Before Matt could ask any more questions, the two men came to the scratch line and faced each other. Then, the bout began. The noise from the onlookers rose, then fell, as the fighters slowly circled, eyeball fixing eyeball, neither willing to make the initial move. For a full minute, they moved around the ring, like two animals, each waiting for the other's concentration to break. The tension built again and the yard grew restless.

"Hit the fucker, why don't you?" someone at the back suddenly yelled, and the shouting from all sides resumed. Smith moved slowly, crabbing sidewards, getting the measure of his opponent. O'Sullivan meanwhile stepped quickly to the left, then to the right, tempting the Englishman to throw the first punch. With no action in the opening moments, the mood of the crowd, William thought, was becoming as ugly as that inside the ring.

"Hit 'im in the bloody breadbasket; punch the bastard's peepers out!"

Matt allowed himself a chuckle, but William watched in silence – watched as Smith circled slowly, ominously, jabbing and lunging, finally making contact with the other man's mouth. The crack of knuckle on bone was followed immediately by cries of support from all parts of the yard. O'Sullivan shook his head, grinned, then spat out a tooth before careering again towards his bigger rival. Getting in close, he suddenly brought his head up, smashing into the underside of Smith's chin with a crunch; the Londoner grunted once before stumbling backwards and falling heavily into the crowd.

"Fuck off back to the ring!" an old scrap of a woman screamed and pushed him away hard, supporters of both sides laughing, egging her on.

Smith rubbed his chin, cursed the woman as a witch, then put up his fists and returned to the line where O'Sullivan was waiting. A second later, both were lashing out again, swinging wild punches that failed to land until, at last, as Smith's arms tired and dropped, his opponent got inside the Londoner's longer reach and landed punch after punch to his torso. Winded and struggling to breathe, Smith finally fell to his knees – O'Sullivan took a step back, and as he stood taunting his adversary, the crowd went wild with excitement.

"Why doesn't he finish the bugger off?" Matt shouted towards William.

"Broughton Rules: can't hit him when he's down."

Disappointed, Matt watched again as Smith got to his feet and launched himself at O'Sullivan, both men taking blows to their heads until their eyebrows and noses bled freely, with blood, saliva, and phlegm flecking their faces and chests, showering those near the edge of the ring.

"Got to hand it to him, Will, Smith's a tough 'un," shouted Matt again; William nodded his agreement.

Round after round passed, and as the lights began to gutter, the two men tired. It was late, and some of the crowd lay on their backs, themselves insensible, knocked out by the cheap liquor and the heat of the bout. A few had started to wander off, but for the most, passions continued to run high, with worsening imprecations heaping themselves on the principals in the ring.

William, tiring too, turned to Matt and yawned theatrically.

"I think I've seen enough for one night. Back to our good ladies?"

Matt nodded, but as they made their way towards the entrance, a loud shout went up – the Londoner had landed a hay-maker that had sent O'Sullivan reeling backwards, to land, eyelids flickering and limbs twitching, at the feet of Smith's supporters. The Irishman's second immediately jumped into the ring indicating that it was all over for his man, and the master of ceremonies re-appeared, shoving his way through to lift the victor's hand and declare him the winner. Smith strode slowly, arrogantly, around the edge of the ring, gesturing to the crowd, the English portion of which was jigging and cheering whilst the Irish booed weakly and cursed, counting their losses as they headed for home. At that moment, through a mist of blood and sweat, Smith's gaze fell upon William and the fighter stood, unmoving, knowing that William was now one step closer to understanding him. William held his stare, nodded once, and steered Matt back to the street.

The walk to the Parkers' cottage took them through the back-streets of Sydney, past more bodies lying sprawled at the side of the road, past more couples making love in the shadows, past more of their own kind wending their slow way home. They walked a sinuous path, arms around shoulders, as much for support as in friendship. They chatted and laughed, shadow boxed the bout's final round, and sang whichever words they could remember from the ballads of earlier on. Not far from home, William jumped out of the road as a cart, stacked high with illicit spirits, clattered by, the driver cursing and shaking his fist at the drunken pair. At last, they arrived at the door.

"Remember to duck your head, Matt," William slurred, as he pressed on the latch and tiptoed into the house. Mary and Daisy were sitting together on the bench, two half-drunk bottles of beer, between them. They stared at the men as they came in.

"Ah, so our heroes return," said Mary, "and how was fair Sydney town tonight?"

"Quiet, as usual?" added Daisy, eyeing Matt up and down.

Matt looked at William quizzically, then leant unsteadily on the edge of the table.

William shrugged, tried to keep his face serious.

"Quite quiet. A fight, bit of music and singing, *plenty* of mating, and just a crazy wagoner to speak of. Nothing more, eh Matt?"

"Nothing more," Matt nodded earnestly.

"Right, let's get you home, Matthew Hodges," Daisy said, then stood up and gave Mary a squeeze. She wagged her finger, "And remember," she mouthed, "look after yourself!"

"I will." Mary smiled, returning the hug.

William waved the guests goodnight, and let Mary walk them to the corner. When she returned, William was face down on the bench, the heave of his shoulders telling her he was fast asleep.

"Good night, my hero, sleep tight," she whispered into his ear. Then, kissing him on the cheek, she made her way to the bedroom alone.

Early next morning, Mary gently shook William awake. He rolled over, yawned, and blinked his sight back into focus. He was not in bed, and the room swam before his eyes.

"'Morning Mary." He sat up, then immediately collapsed back onto the bench, holding his hands to his temples. "What did I have to drink, last night?"

"I have no idea, Will. That's something you are going to have to ask Matthew Hodges…but I doubt if he'll be able to answer, either, the way he was rolling as they started for home. One day, you're going to have to realise that you are not as young as you were."

"I'm not *old*, Mary, I'm…" he struggled to remember.

"Well, there you are, that proves it. You can't even remember your own age! And anyway, it's not all about birthdays – it's more about growing up, being a man, having responsibilities."

William propped himself up on an elbow and looked over to where she was sitting, demurely, hands in her lap. He furrowed his brow and attempted to formulate another question. "And… um…what news from Daisy?"

"*Daisy? News?* None to speak of. More *my* news for her."

William narrowed his eyes.

"Your news? For Daisy?"

"Yes Will," she said, standing up; and smiling coyly at his confusion, snuggled in beside him.

12

The *Earl Cornwallis* had come and gone, its cargo of tea now safely stored in the adjoining warehouse, in the back-office of which William and Mac sat slumped. The other workers had departed an hour earlier. Their boss was late. William yawned and let his hand glide over the smooth leather surface of the chair, so unlike anything either he, or his workmates, would ever have in their own homes.

"You look done in. Just the promise of impending fatherhood too much, is it?"

William shook his head.

"It's been a hard day, Mac. And yes, yesterday's news did come as a bit of a shock."

"How long to go?"

"About six months – maybe seven," said William, "I'm not quite sure."

"Ah well, you'll have some way to go to match Mick and his woman, and he still manages a good day's work."

William said nothing, then sat up straighter.

"I was out on Saturday with an old mucker – Matt – a rare night out, at the Red Cow –"

"Aye, I've heard of it," Mac interrupted with a grin.

"I'm sure you have, but listen – the yard at the back, well, it doubles up as a ring, for boxing."

Mac nodded.

"And two nights ago, who should I see fighting there but –"

Mac's hand shot up, and he looked around quickly.

"Wheesht! Keep your voice down. I know who you're going to say. But we don't want Mr Campbell getting wind of it."

William lowered his voice.

"So…Smith, then? He's a regular?"

"You could say that. And Mr Campbell, God-fearing man that he is, would have him out on his ear if he got to know. All the gamblin' and cursin', you understand, Mr Parker."

William sat back.

"*And*," Mac whispered, forcing William to lean closer, "Smith has *friends* – supporters, who make a pretty penny from his exploits; the sort of friends you would not want to upset, if you follow my meaning."

"I think I do, Mac," said William, just as the door creaked open and their employer walked in.

"Ah, gentlemen – no, don't stand up, I can see you've both had a hard day. I've just been to the warehouse, and it's full to bursting. Well done. Can I get you something? Tea, perhaps?"

"Very kind of you, Mr Campbell," Mac said, a grin cracking his face, "but no – it wouldn't trouble me if I never saw another tea leaf as long as I live."

They laughed and Campbell took his seat behind the desk. Readjusting his spectacles, he shuffled some papers then selected a letter from the top of the pile.

"I have here a letter from a friend and business associate of mine from up country – a Mr Gregory Blaxland. Mac knows him well. You have heard of him, perhaps?"

William shook his head.

Campbell walked over to a map hanging from a board, squinted closely at the detail, then laid his finger on a point towards the extreme left-hand edge.

"Mr Blaxland is a landowner of some importance, and has a large farmstead here on the Emu Plain, about two days west and north of Sydney, beyond Parramatta. He has substantial numbers of both sheep and cattle and it is of the latter I need to speak to you now. A consignment of a hundred and fifty head is due to arrive at the wharf, sometime in the next two, three months – it depends on the weather – and he has employed me, that is, us, to assist him in driving them from ship to farm. And that, Mr Parker, is where you come in. I need you to deliver them safely to Blaxland, ably assisted of course by Mac here – he's done this several times before – and any other men we decide that you need. So, you'll be away for three, maybe four, days in total – have either of you any questions?"

William turned to look at Mac, then back to his boss who was watching him expectantly from over his glasses.

"A hundred and fifty head, you say? That seems quite a number to me. How many men will I be able to take along?"

"With you and Mac, another three or four should suffice. There are always others able to take your places here at the wharf, albeit on a temporary basis – the Captain will see to that."

"And, what route should we take. Is there a drovers' road all the way?"

Campbell returned to the map and traced out a line.

"You start here, at the wharf, and follow the river as far as Parramatta, or just outside, where you can overnight. You'll be met by one of Blaxland's men who will guide you this way, westward, until you reach the Emu Plains, and Blaxland's farm. We can go into greater detail nearer the time, when the ship has been sighted and we know when she's due. So," Campbell said, checking his watch, "I'll bid you good-night – it's late and you must be tired."

William and Mac left the office, walked through the warehouse and stopped on the street outside. It was dark and the wharf was almost empty, just a few stragglers making their way home at the end of a long day.

"We'll have a bit of an adventure," said Mac, reassuring, "A day following the river, and a night near Parramatta before we head off across the plains to the west. Should be interesting. And don't worry, Mr Parker, you can tell that woman of yours that I'll make sure we come home safely."

"Thanks Mac – and when we're not in the office, it's Will."

Mac placed a fatherly hand on his shoulder, bade him goodnight, then headed off in the direction of home.

Will turned and made off towards his Pitt Street lodgings. Head down and hands in pockets, he was deep in thought – excited at the prospect of the journey to Blaxland's farm and flattered by the trust placed in him by Campbell; but also, anxious about the new responsibilities he had unexpectedly inherited. Suddenly, a figure stepped out of the shadows, waking him from his reverie.

"Mr Parker…good-evening to you."

A tall, well-built man stood before him, blocking his way. William peered through the gloom, smelled the rum filling the air.

"Smith? What do you want, and what do you think you're doing jumping out on me like that?"

William made to walk past, but Smith stepped to the side, blocking him again.

"Cosy chat with Mr Campbell, was it? You and Mac?"

"What do you mean? And what business is it of yours?"

"That's just it – I don't want any business of mine bandied about between people it don't concern. If you follow me, Sir."

William looked around him. On the corner, a shadowy figure appeared, his face faintly illuminated by the smoky glow of a full pipe, then another across the street.

"Look, Smith, I'm not interested in your… pugilistic activities –"

"Big words, Mr Parker," Smith interrupted.

"– just as long as they don't interfere with your work at the wharf. In fact –"

Smith held up a large hand.

"Then that's good, it seems we understand each other, 'cos there's a lot of people who would not appreciate you saying anything that might upset their boy, stop him from persuin' his legitimate interests, if you know what I mean?"

"Yes. I do know what you mean, Smith. Now, I'll bid you goodnight."

Smith stepped slowly and deliberately out of his way and he started to walk again. The two other men disappeared into the night as William, glancing once over his shoulder, hurried his way back home; to Mary, and their unborn child.

13

It was Monday night, the end of another long day. Blaxland's cattle would be another month, and Mary was getting bigger. William walked alone, clutching a small bag of provisions he'd bought from the government store on George Street. The night had fallen quickly and a cold wind was building. Some sparse heat, and the only light, leaked from the few braziers which jostled for supremacy with the long dark shadows of the street. All around, the pubs were full of those who had managed to save a little, who were now drowning their sorrows in rum and cheap ale. And as he navigated his way through the streets and alleys, the sights and sounds of a callow young colony, finding its feet, closed in on him: the gambling dens, the prostitutes, the swell of patriotic songs rising dangerously above the curses and the threats. Men drinking themselves into a stupor. William pulled up his collar and hurried along. He thought of Mary, at home, preparing the fire on which to cook their evening meal – then it began, rattling the air like a thunderclap announcing a storm.

From nowhere, from everywhere, the Irish appeared, bearing arms. They carried hammers and knives, but most of all pikes. William stepped quickly into the shadows as the bars and the brothels emptied, decanting their dregs into the once empty street. The throng, growing larger and angrier, roared their defiance to the night. "Death or Liberty!" they cried, as William watched in silence. And around him they rushed, like a river round a rock, tripping over their own feet, knocking each other and the braziers to the ground. One of the men – he thought he recognised him – grabbed a firebrand and tossed it into an open doorway, then wheeled away, whooping, as the flimsy wooden building exploded, briefly turning night into day.

William dragged himself further into the darkness and cowered beneath the veranda of the nearest building, making himself small, wanting to disappear. He watched as a breakaway gang, a dozen or so convicts, suddenly appeared opposite where he lay, holding their pikes aloft, screaming their challenge to the soldiers whose barracks were a mere stone's throw away. He watched for a minute or two, mutely, and listened as their drunken voices reached fever pitch, the vitriol against their masters becoming ever more poisonous.

"Will ye not come out and face us yer feckin' cowards?" he heard one scream, "Is His Majesty's militia afeared of a bunch of Micks?" another. Then a flash from the darkness, followed immediately by a scream and the thud of a body hitting the ground. Then another flash before the group dispersed, scattering this way, then that, like sheep before the wolf.

The shots brought yet more men onto the streets, most of them heaping Irish curses onto the heads of the uniformed soldiers whose numbers, William noted, were also swelling by the second. Whistles blared, drums rolled, and a bell sounded urgently in a cacophony that served to deepen the confusion still further. A sudden squall swept the street as William watched more and more groups pouring in around him, like flood-water: from George Street, West Market Street, and from the direction of the wharves, men armed with pikes and any other tools on which they could lay their hands. The rioters had come prepared – this attack was planned. A noise from behind and William turned suddenly; a body of soldiers was now blocking the exit from George Street, hurriedly forming themselves into two untidy ranks, the back row standing and the front row on their knees. Above the tumult, William heard an English voice, desperate, trying to impose some order; and then the order to fire. A volley shattered the night air and more convict bodies slumped to the ground. William watched the group, enraged and fuelled by drink, as they charged again; but turned his head away as a rioter in the van thrust his pike into the chest of a fresh-faced soldier who was trying to re-load, before he too was killed, by a pistol shot, point-blank, to the head. William clutched his bag to his chest and closed his eyes. When he opened them again, it was to see a pair of convicts breaking cover towards him, backs bent, keeping low, before they were stopped dead in their tracks, caught in a grey hail of lead. The pair fell a few feet from where he hid, a bloodied hand stretching out across the ground, towards the post of the veranda, like that of a drowning man. William lay flat on his front, managed to grasp the twitching fingers, and through the darkness made out what would be the man's final words: whispers to his "mammy", that he loved her. When at last the hand went limp, William retreated into his corner and forced himself to think straight, forced himself to quell the pounding of his heart drowning out the tiny voice of reason that was trying to be heard. He breathed deeply, considered what to do next. The man was dead and his friend lay sprawled, unmoving, across the other's legs. There was no hope.

With his hands to his head, he scanned the scene and tried to remember, remember which alleyways would lead him to the Tank

Stream, and home, and which were dead-ends – the word caught in his throat. Forcing himself to concentrate, he counted the openings between the buildings, which he whispered out-loud, to himself: Thomas Wyatt's house, Joshua Wright's house, Solomon's Bar…his gaze finally fixing on the one opening he was looking for – the alleyway that led down to the stream, and then on to the garden, and back to Mary. Mary! The thought hit him like a bullet in his chest. Was she still alive? Or had some madman thrown a burning brand into *their* house too? He came to his senses, wrestling with the confusion that swirled around his head. He crouched, then darted across the street – wide and exposed – to the far side where a group of pike carriers barrelled into him, knocking him flat. They paid him little heed – the blood of a fellow convict was not the prize they sought as they roared past, on this cold winter's night, towards the sound of soldiers.

William wiped the sweat from his eyes, and from behind the shelter of the post peered into the blackness again. The street seemed to be emptying, the clamour of threats and counter-threats fading as the soldiers' white crosses disappeared into the murk. William made a short burst for the next building, then, when he was sure it was safe, ran for the alleyway. Looking back once, he darted into the void between the two buildings, then stopped abruptly a few paces later – it led nowhere. He cursed, then turned to face the faint glow of the street he'd left behind, edging his way back to where he had started. As he neared the street he froze, held his breath again, and could hear nothing but the swoosh of blood in his ears. The entrance to the alley was blocked, and towering above him, barring his way, stood a huge silhouette, pike in hand. It ambled menacingly towards him, blocking out more of the light. Both men stopped, and then the other spoke.

"Well, if it isn't the feckin' canal boy. Out all alone are ye? 'Tis a dangerous night to be out, alone."

William could not see the face but knew the voice only too well. "O'Connor?" He dropped his bag, felt his legs turn to butter.

"Indeed, it is, Mr Parker. Didn't bank on seeing me again, did yeh?"

William made no answer.

The sudden flash of an explosion, from somewhere nearby, illuminated the big man, and for a moment William glimpsed the familiar thin smile that played across his face. In the background, the sounds of voices were coming nearer – rebel voices, and the voices of soldiers shouting, telling them to drop their pikes or be shot. Like a cornered animal, William crabbed slowly from one side of the alley to the other, looking for any opportunity to escape; then caught the reek of stale beer that filled the air between them, and thought he saw O'Connor sway a little on his feet.

"You're not going anywhere, son," O'Connor said darkly, and raised his pike.

William looked round for anything, anything he could use as a weapon – a stone or a branch – and finding nothing, crouched down to scoop up a handful of dust.

O'Connor moved towards him, slowly, his pike now levelled at William, jabbing it forwards, thrusting it at his chest. William backed off, fixing his eyes all the time on the swaying figure. O'Connor spat, then with a sudden roar swung out, in a wide arc towards his head. Like a boxer ducking inside his opponent's reach, William threw the dust with all his strength towards the other's eyes. As O'Connor's hand went to his face, the pike flailed round and William felt his head explode.

"Yuh Bastard, yuh. I'll skewer ye like the pig y'are!" he heard O'Connor say as he reached out, trying to locate him. William pulled clear, scrambling on all fours into the faint light of the street, as the blood continued to pour into his eyes. He staggered blindly to his feet then froze as he felt a huge hand grabbing him by the collar, felt it dragging him back…then covered his face, and waited for the end.

When the musket ball hit, The Big Fellah dropped, in an instant, like one of the giant trees they had felled together in times gone by. The ground shuddered briefly; then the world stood still.

William, unsure of what had happened, sat with his eyes closed tight, then looked up to see a soldier skidding to a halt, bayonette pointing directly at O'Connor's stomach. He was even younger than himself, William noted, and his face was pale with shock.

"Halt! Put your 'ands in the air!" he screamed at William, by this time sitting on his haunches a pace or two from the body.

William thrust his arms awkwardly to the sky believing again that he was about to die, but the soldier lowered his weapon, then shouted at him to explain who he was and what he was doing out.

"I am William Parker, Sir, out to buy provisions from the government store. I mean you no harm!"

Noting his accent, the soldier adjusted his chin-strap and straightened his hat before motioning to William that he should leave the shadows and make himself scarce.

"Piss off 'ome, mate. And don't stop for nothin'."

Obeying the order, William scrambled to his feet and ran. Ran to the next alleyway – the alley he'd been searching for – then ran down the hill to the Tank Stream which, by the light of a watery moon, pointed the way back to his garden, to Mary, and to safety.

14

"So, you survived?" Mac's face was serious.

"I *survived*," said William, "but only just. If that Redcoat hadn't come along…"

"Aye, well he did. Can't begrudge yourself just *one* favour from the buggers. It'll be a while before you get another."

William pulled hard on the rope and tightened the knot securing the bundle to the back of the wagon, and Mac checked it before nodding.

"That'll do, Will. Time for them to be moving out."

William called over to where a man was taking a pipe, resting on one of the many wooden bollards lining the quay.

"All done, Joshua, you can take them away."

The bullocky looked over and emptied his pipe, tapping it on the post. He was a surly-looking man, a cabbage-tree hat pulled over his ears, a dirty twill shirt and moleskin trousers.

"Looks happy," said William.

Mac just smiled then shouted, "And don't you go givin' the bulls here a hard time Josh, you've a long road ahead of yous."

The man didn't smile back, and spat on his hand.

"Alright for you, Jock. Nice little house to go home to, nice wife maybe, but me…" he cracked his whip into the dust, "me? Got fuck all, apart from this lot."

"Aye, be that as it may. Get yourself movin' now. And God speed."

William got out of the way as the man took his place at the left side of the bullock team. A young boy, his off-sider, joined him on the right. Another crack from the long whip and the team of four started their slow way along the quay. It would be days before they reached their destination.

William and Mac watched as Joshua and his cart departed.

"And how's Mary?"

"Let's take five minutes," William said, and gestured to Mac that he should sit on a pile of sacks that was to be their next job. "She's worried, Mac. Scared that O'Connor's men will come and finish off what he started."

"And will they? Would they chase you, down here?"

William shrugged.

"I hope not. But who knows?"

"Can't see it, really. Things move on, and they'll find other fish to fry. And by the way, there's no need for you to be troubling yourself with all this heavy work. That's what the boss pays the likes of *them* to do." He pointed at the stevedores and others in Campbell's employ, "You're supposed to be in charge."

William laughed. "I know Mac, I know. But I'm not a pen and paper man – never was, never will be. I like to get my hands dirty. The canals didn't dig themselves."

Another bullock cart trundled by, the bullocky lifting his hat and shouting a cheery good morning.

"So, they're not all like Joshua then, Mac."

"Ach, he's a miserable bugger, but it's a tough life on the road – not one I'd want for mysel'."

At that moment, a loud bang echoed across the quay, followed by the sound of two men arguing. William craned his neck – it was Mick and Smith. A large barrel lay on its side, the liquid contents spilling onto the ground. The air was filled with shouting and swearing, both men gesticulating and waving their arms angrily.

"Better get over there, now," said William, and both ran to where the other two continued to shout.

"Smith, Mick, cut it out. Now!" William kept his voice calm and level.

"That stupid fu–" Smith stopped himself mid-word. His face was red and hot, blue veins bulging clearly on his shaven head, "he dropped the fuckin' barrel! Again!"

He swung round, an eight-inch cargo hook held above his shoulder, like a weapon ready to strike.

"Smithy, put the hook down. There's a good lad." Mac took a step towards him, his hands raised. "Come on, son. Give me the hook."

Smith stood, staring at Mac, his hand shaking, then brought the hook down hard, burying it in the side of the barrel at his feet.

Mac breathed out, let his hands drop.

"He's a fuckin' idiot. Doesn't know one end of a barrel from the other." Smith's eyes continued to stare, his hand shaking as he pointed directly at his workmate. Then turning to William, "So, what are you going to do about it, *Sir*, or how many more effin' barrels are we going to lose?" He stopped; the hate clear in his eyes.

William pointed, first at Smith, and then at the buildings. "Get to the warehouse. Get on with stacking there. I'll speak to you later. Mick, clear this stuff up, then get yourself home. I'll see you in the morning."

Smith made to say something, looked at Mac, then turned on his heel and went. Mick nodded, dusted himself down, then quietly set about clearing up the mess of the broken barrel.

The rest of the afternoon passed without incident, and as they prepared to finish for the day, William and Mac were chatting.

"So, what do you advise, Mac?"

"Och, he's a hot temper, but I think I know how to handle him." Mac avoided William's gaze. "Just leave him to me, I'll deal with this."

"No, Mac, that's not going to solve it. What did you say? *You're supposed to be in charge,* so that's what I'll do – be in charge."

Mac nodded. "Well, if that's what you want. But I will come along with you."

Ten minutes later, they were in the warehouse office. Smith, hands on his hips, was staring at William.

"So, have you calmed down Smith?" William was standing with his hands behind his back, breathing slowly, steadily.

Smith jolted his head upwards and remained silent.

"I'll take that as a yes. Until further notice, you are to work in the warehouse. Stay away from the quay, stay away from Mick. You'll report to Mr Doyle – is that right, Mac?"

Mac nodded.

"And in the event of any further trouble, it will be Mr Campbell you will be speaking to, not me. Do I make myself clear?"

"Perfectly clear. *Sir.*"

"Good. Now get out."

Smith glanced once in the direction of Mac then left the room, slamming the door behind him. The two men stood quietly until William broke the silence.

"Mac?"

"Aye, you did the right thing. I dinnae think you'll be hearing from Smith for a while now. I'll have a word with Doyle, so he's in the picture."

"Thank you, Mac, that would be a help."

As they turned to leave, the door swung open and Mr Campbell walked in.

"Gentlemen? Didn't expect to find you *here.* Is everything alright?"

"Yes, Mr Campbell, just a little altercation that I had to sort out. Nothing to worry about."

"That's splendid, William, splendid. And I have some good news: *The Valiant* has been sighted, two days from The Heads, which means Mr Blaxland's cattle will be with us soon. You need to be ready to leave by the end of the week."

15

William pulled back on the reins, bringing his horse to a welcomed halt. He reached for his canteen and drank down to the last drop of water – even this late in the day, the heat was unbearable.

"Well done, *Star*, we're nearly there."

A little way off, Mac removed his hat and shouted. "This is the spot, Will. We'll let them eat and drink, then we'll set up camp and stop for the night."

A hundred and fifty head of Mr Blaxland's newly acquired cattle would need little coaxing to descend the bank, then drink from the river that had been their guide since just before daybreak. From the moment they left, the sun had poured down; the clear blue sky, no protection, standing stark against the red dust of the parched ground – they all were in need of a rest.

Mac shouted again, gesticulating to the stockmen riding at the flanks of the mob. They stopped, guiding the cattle down to the edge of the river, where the animals started to drink their fill or hungrily nuzzled the sparse vegetation clinging to the banks – this, after all, was Australia, not the lush pastures of their English homeland. Midstream, two men and their horses looked on while their dogs rested, their heads on their paws; exhausted, but eager to do their duty if called upon.

Parramatta, Australia's second town, was just around the bend, evidenced by the wisps of grey-blue smoke ascending slowly into an evening sky that was now turning crimson. William took off his hat and batted at the swarm of mosquitoes plaguing humans and animals alike. He rode closer to Mac.

"I'll look after the cattle, Mac; you can deal with the bloody flies."

"If only I could, Will, but I'm no magician. Reminds me of summers back in Scotland. It's enough to drive us all – the beasts included – right out of our heads."

On cue, a bull bellowed at the rising moon, shaking its huge head in frustration.

"Right, that settles it," said Mac. "Time to move them. Away from the river; when the sun goes down, we might get some relief from these blasted midges."

A series of whistles, shouts and waves told the rest of the gang of their intentions. The smell of dung carried on the breeze as the mob came together and moved slowly, complaining, up the slope, and away from the water. For the first time that day William became aware of the incessant lowing and of the rumble of hooves on the bone-dry ground. Sitting astride *Star*, his horse for the week, he watched as Mac and the men brought order and shape to the scene before him – whatever his own job title was, it was Mac who was in charge. A whoop here, the dart of a dog there, and the mob began to move as one. What had started as seven score beasts and ten, each inclined to eat, drink and dally as the mood would take them, was now a single herd, like children, walking together hand in hand on a Sunday evening stroll.

With the cattle moved, the camp set up, and the evening meal eaten, they settled down for the night. The smell of cooking lingered in the still night air, mingling with the astringent whiff of cheap tobacco. William and Mac spread out their swags near each other while the others positioned themselves at various points around the animals. Mac reached into a large burlap bag, and on the ground between them laid a rifle, covering it lightly with a cloth.

"Have you ever used one of these things, Will?"

William shook his head.

"We're trusted; but it's just in case, you understand – strictly bushrangers or natives. Or dingoes."

William said nothing, but nodded.

"Well, it'll be another long day tomorrow so we'd best get some shut-eye."

"Won't be easy to sleep in this heat, and I'm saddle sore too, but goodnight anyway," Will yawned.

"Night Will – and you did well today," Mac added wearily, muttering a few closing words into the ground before he fell silent.

Despite the night heat, and to a chorus of deep bellowing, William fell asleep quickly, waking only to slap at any one of the many nocturnal visitors that nipped at carelessly exposed flesh. As the dawn broke, he opened his eyes briefly and listened. In addition to the noise of cattle he could hear the low rumblings of distant thunder, faint but getting louder. He propped himself up, stiff and uncomfortable on the hard ground, and watched as the first rays of the day reached high into the sky. It was going to be another hot one. Faraway, he saw the unmistakable flash of lightning, then another roll of thunder. And then, nothing. He waited, closed his eyes, then fell back into a shallow slumber.

Suddenly, as if the rifle itself had gone off, a loud crack rent the air. Will and Mac leapt out of their swags looking around for what, or who, had assaulted them. Above them, thunderclouds billowed, and nearby a solitary gumtree had burst into flame. The air was thick with dust and a deep rumbling shook the earth…the cattle were now on the move, and heading towards Parramatta.

"Will!" Mac screamed above the mounting noise, "We've got to head them off. They'll flatten the town!"

Without thinking, William grabbed at the gun and ran for his horse. In seconds, he was moving at full-tilt, galloping alongside the bellowing, snorting mob that with every moment was closing in on Parramatta's outlying cottages. Clouds of dust blinded him as hundreds of hooves pounded the dry ground. With the smell of fear filling his nose and his mouth, William dug his heels into *Star's* flanks, urging her on, in a race against time, to catch the leading steers that were now three hundred yards ahead. He could hear nothing bar the thundering of the cattle but, looking across, caught a glimpse of another horseman galloping east – at least he was not alone. Wiping his eyes, he caught sight of something that made him gasp: a smallholding, one of the many marking the limits of the nearby town, was getting closer with every moment; a second look nearly made him sick – tiny figures scurrying to all sides, running for their lives. He was now gaining on the leading group, *Star* living up to her name. Second by second, the scene up ahead was becoming clearer, more people appearing, more people running, to the left, to the right, in a desperate bid to avoid the awful death that standing still would surely bring.

"Faster, *Star*, faster!" William screamed in her ear and the horse responded with another, perhaps her only remaining, burst of speed. Now, William could make out the figures, see them for what they really were: men in large hats, women grasping babies to their breasts, small wailing children standing like statues, left to fend for themselves. *Star* was level with the leading bulls, and now William could see the fear, the blind panic in their eyes. They were seconds from disaster when William fired the gun, high into the air. The sharp report echoed through the bush and the mob changed direction, away from the noise, away from the good people of Parramatta. The bulls at the front veered sharply and almost lost their footing as they skidded, turned, then retreated into the distance, away from where William and *Star* had slowed, then stopped, exhausted. Another gunshot and the mob was starting to run in a circle, excited dogs adding their barks to the shouts of the men forced to pull their horses up and away from the panicking herd. Slowly, the leading animals started to tire, their lowing, and the barking of excited dogs, began to abate, and the calm of the previous evening gradually resumed. Ten minutes after it had started, the animals were walking back towards the camp, turning their backs on the town by whose inhabitants they had never been invited to visit. Above them, the heavens grumbled, but no raindrops reached the ground, the warm air quickly turning them back into the thin clouds from which they had come. Then, with the cattle, no worse for their experience, feeding on whatever they could find, the men were soon packing up camp.

"That was a close thing, Will," Mac said, drinking his tea.

"Certainly was, Mac. And I promised Mary it wouldn't be dangerous."

"Aye, well…these things happen in the bush. But you did well with the gun. Who taught you that?"

"*You* did Mac – it was the last thing you said as you dropped off to sleep last night. You don't remember?"

"Can't say that I do," he said scratching his head, "but I'm mightily relieved that *one* of us did."

At that point, one of the stockmen shouted across that a group of horses and men had been spotted and were heading their way, coming in from the west.

"That'll be Blaxland's men. Probably just as well they missed all the fun," said Mac.

They did not have long to wait before the men joined them. A small man, with thick dark hair and a badly broken nose, stepped forward.

"Sean Galvin! It's great to see you. Long time, no see," Mac said as he greeted him. "I was hoping it might be you."

"Sure, and it's grand to see you too, Mac. You're looking younger than when I saw you last."

Mac smiled, almost embarrassed.

"And this is Mr Parker – Will," he added, looking for his boss's approval.

"Pleased to meet you, Mr Galvin." William gestured to the cattle grazing nearby. "Well, here they are. Mr Blaxland's new acquisitions. How many hours to their new home?"

The new arrival stood with his hands on his hips, casting an expert eye over the mob grazing contentedly nearby. He said nothing for a few seconds, doing the calculations, then told William that, all things being equal, they should be at the farm by mid-afternoon.

"So – an uneventful journey, I take it?" he said.

William looked over at Mac and nodded, giving him permission to relate what had happened; so recent that the dust was still settling on their heads and shoulders.

"Aye, well, uneventful is not how we would put it, eh Will?" Galvin looked at Will, then back at Mac.

"If it hadn't been for the quick thinking of William, here, parts of Parramatta would be no more. The mob rushed, just after daybreak. See that tree? Lightning strike."

Galvin looked over at the still smouldering trunk and understood.

"And God knows where the cattle would have ended up," Mac concluded.

"Seems Mr Blaxland, and the residents of Parramatta, are in your debt. Well done," Galvin said, and shook William's hand for a second time.

"Well," said William, resuming his place as boss, "We should be making tracks. Get them moving while it's still morning. I take it you know the way, Sean?"

"That, I certainly do," he replied with a wry smile, then called in his men to help drive the cattle, westwards, and to their new home.

Gregory Blaxland was waiting at the farm boundary when word got to him that the mob had been seen crossing the South Creek. Galvin led as they rounded a bluff and made their way slowly through the remaining few acres of open plain before crossing into Blaxland's property. Spotting his boss, he raised his hat and waved, Blaxland doing the same in reply. Minutes later, William joined Galvin as they brought the animals to a stop, dogs and men working together to finally bring the cattle home. It had been a long journey; twelve thousand miles, by land – then sea – then land again.

While Blaxland's men dealt with the new arrivals, the men from Sydney washed away the grime of the past two days, then sat and ate with their host. And then it was time to make the journey home. Blaxland and Galvin rode out as far as the creek.

"It's been good to see you again, Mac," said Blaxland. "Give my regards to Mr Campbell. The cattle look in need of fattening up, but otherwise appear to be what I expected. And young Parker, I appreciate what you did this morning; an astounding bit of riding I was told."

William looked abashed, but acknowledged the compliment with a nod.

"And, when you are able, if you ever need a new position, well, I am always on the lookout for good stockmen. And with a hundred and fifty more cattle to look after…" he left the sentence unfinished. "So, I'll bid you farewell and a safe journey back to Sydney."

With a final wave, they disappeared behind the bluff and rode till they reached the very spot where they had slept the previous night. Without the cattle, the atmosphere was relaxed as the men made up a simple camp and set a small fire on which to cook a meal and get the billy boiling. It also kept away the dingoes and the mosquitoes – or so the theory went.

Sitting around the fire, William and the men ate, drank, and swapped their stockmen's tales. To the accompaniment of an old fiddle they sang, badly – mainly drovers' songs but also songs of love and reminiscence. And as the grog and the day took their toll, one by one the men peeled off until just William and Mac were left.

William threw another log into the flames and watched as a shower of sparks filled the air.

"Mac, you don't seem yourself tonight. Quiet. Not singing. Are you alright?"

Mac took another swig of rum and stared into the flames, his eyes distant and rheumy.

"I'm fine."

"Fine?"

"Aye, fine. Just fine and dandy."

"Is there something you want to tell me, Mac?"

"No!" Mac shouted, then immediately hung his head. "Smith."

"Smith? What about Smith?"

"I seen him."

"In the Red Cow?"

Mac jumped unsteadily to his feet. "No! *Not* in the Red Cow," he slurred, waving the bottle in William's face. "I seen him with his *father*," he added, his eyes suddenly opening up wide, as if he was seeing it all again.

"But Smith's father's dead, Mac, you're not making –"

"He *killed* him. He did his father in…pushed him under the ox cart." Mac fell forward as he pushed at thin air, almost landing in the fire. William grabbed at his arm and helped him to sit down again, where he remained, staring morosely at his feet.

"*Killed* him? You *saw* him kill his own father?"

Mac let the bottle drop and nodded gravely, miming again the push that had done for Smith senior.

"Then, Mac, he's a murderer. You know what we have to do."

16

It was a Sunday, the colony's day of rest, and William and Matt had found a place where they could sit and talk alone, as friends. Walking near the top of the area known as The Rocks, the tower of Fort Phillips just behind them, they stopped to rest on a large boulder, hewn from nearby sandstone cliffs. From their vantage point they could see the coast on one side stretching south towards Botany Bay, on the other, to areas hardly as yet explored. Below them lay half a dozen boats at anchor, their flags fluttering in the northerly breeze; and beyond the cove, Government House and gardens, flanked by narrow streets which stretched like a fallen ladder to the outer edges of the expanding town. Matt pointed out the dark blue line of hills just visible on the western horizon, then turned to William.

"So, what was it like, Will? The trial."

William shook his head and took a moment before answering.

"Bloody awful, Matt. When it happened to *me* – my trial – it was like a dream, and I couldn't really take it all in; but being there, being a witness, and having to speak…" he shook his head again, "it just made it all more real somehow."

"What about Mac? He was the prime witness I suppose, wasn't he?"

"The *only* witness to the actual killing, or so they said. Strange, in a busy area of the quay, in the middle of the working day, that nobody else saw a thing," William said with a sardonic smile. "All too frightened of Smith and his cronies, so they turned their backs and walked away. The old John Smith was no more popular than his son, so any other witnesses suddenly went deaf and blind."

"So, what did he say – Mac? And what about Smith himself? Did he deny it?"

"Smith? Did he hell! He stood there, with his chest pushed out, and grinned. His father was just another opponent, put on his back, now dead to the world. Except, in his case, he wasn't going to come round again. And when he was told to speak, Smith spoke like I had never heard him before. You know, he wasn't the greatest talker and would dry up after spitting out the first few sentences, but in front of the court he sounded like an orator."

Matt angled his head, "Really? Saying what exactly?"

"It was sad. His father had been a complete bastard towards him. He taught him how to box; but only by punching him black and blue. He'd learned the hard way how to look after himself and did exactly what his father taught him, I suppose. And in the end, old John went down just like all the others who crossed his son. Smith wasn't the little whipping boy anymore, and the old man paid the price for not understanding that. Shall we carry on walking?"

The pair stood up and started to descend the steep path towards the cove. A group of Cadigal were fishing, like they had since time immemorial. Dressed in their new neighbours' cast-offs, they looked uncomfortable and incongruous, their dark, lean bodies visible beneath oversized jackets and tattered jerkins.

Matt pressed William further.

"You didn't tell me about Mac, Will. Is he alright after all this? And what about you? And Mary."

"Mac is fine," William said, "well, no, not really fine. Smith was a workmate, and he'd known him for years. I don't think Mac liked the father or the son, but he had no choice and had to work with them. Mac is a gentle soul, so I can't say Mac is going to miss either of them, but he's a God-fearing man too, and knew he could not keep quiet about what he had seen. He was confused and frightened, but in the end said what he had to say."

"Which was?"

William looked at Matt and shrugged his shoulders.

"That he'd seen Smith pushing his father under the wheels of the ox cart, of course. That Smith had made no attempt to save his father, and that he had bent down and whispered something to him as he lay on the ground, then turned and walked away calmly, leaving him to die."

"And Smith didn't deny that?" said Matt.

"No. When the judge asked him if this was true, and what he had said, he just laughed and told the court that he'd told his father that he would see him in Hell."

"Which he will."

"Which he will," William agreed.

The two had reached George Street which stretched along the north edge of the cove, past Campbell's Wharf, out to Dawes' Point. William picked up a pebble and shied it across the water, counting the skips until it disappeared silently beneath the surface. One of the fishermen raised his hat and shouted something indecipherable in appreciation of the feat, and William waved back.

They were heading back into town, making their way through the untidy scattering of self-built convict huts and cottages that littered the promontory they had just descended. Groups of natives and convicts were standing listlessly on the corners, when one woman, and then another, called over to Will and Matt from the shadows, inviting them to join them in their doorways. The breeze was picking up and dark clouds were starting to roll in from the open sea.

They were strolling in silence when William suddenly spoke again.

"I'm more concerned about Mac than Mary or myself," William said, aware they were passing the point where old John Smith had breathed his last. "He was the one who had to stand and make his statement. All I needed to do was tell the court that I was with Mac when he told me what had happened, to say a few words about Smith, and how I knew him to be a violent man – you know, about the boxing and about the time when I had to break up the fight between him and Mick on the quayside."

"But Will," said Matt, "Smith's friends are a dangerous lot; a bunch of hardmen and bullies. You need to be careful, for both yourself and Mary's sakes."

William stopped and placed his hands on Matt's shoulders.

"I know. I don't like this any more than the next man, but what am I supposed to do? I have a wife, and a baby on the way. I have to earn a crust and what I do pays better than most. I can't run away from them Matt. And besides, there's nowhere for me to run. As my mother used to say when I was a little boy: it will be all right in the morning."

Matt nodded his head, unconvinced.

"Just take care, Will; and you know you've got friends too, if you need us."

By the time they were ready to part, the rain had started to fall. Matt pulled in his collar and turned to face his friend.

"So, when is the hanging?"

"Tomorrow. At the Gallows Fields. I'll keep Mac company. He'll need someone at his side."

Matt nodded and wished his friend all the best for the following day.

William gave a weak smile, turned, then walked the last half-mile alone.

17

The crowds were gathering, flowing in from all corners of the colony and making their way slowly towards the Gallows Fields. It was unusually quiet, a cold, still day, the columns of smoke from a hundred cottage chimneys rising vertically towards the heavens.

William and Mac stood at a distance, watching their fellow prisoners walk past.

"You did what you had to do, my friend."

"Aye," replied Mac, keeping his voice low, "but it makes it no easier, does it?"

William heaved a sigh.

"No, it makes it no easier. But it was the *right* thing to do, Mac. He'd killed his own father; in cold blood from what you say."

Neither said anything for a few moments.

"Aye. You *are* right, Will," said Mac, resigned, "So, shall we join the rest? I feel a wee bit conspicuous standing here, apart."

The two started in the same direction as the rest, and walked on in silence. All they ever dreamed of was escape, William thought, and now Smith was doing just that. Not by canoe, or by walking blindly into the heat of the bush, but courtesy of the hangman's rope. He shuddered.

"I'm not sure I want to get much closer," William said, as they came within sight of the gallows. "We're still attending – as expected. Let's stop here, out of the way."

Mac nodded and they stood in silence towards the periphery of the throng. Convicts and Redcoats continued to arrive quietly, the mood sombre and dark. Looking around, William became aware of two men peering at them intensely – almost certainly friends of Smith. One pointed – first at William, then at Mac – and smiled, then ran his finger across his throat before turning back towards the low hill on which the gallows waited. Mac had been looking down at his feet; William said nothing to enlighten him.

Smith finally appeared at the front, and a murmur, like an incoming wave, rose, then fell, as the figure of the condemned man was led up to the platform. With his arms tied behind his back, two Redcoats helped him negotiate the steps – the first time, William thought, he had ever been helped by a soldier. People stood on tip-toe, craning to see, while William and Mac flicked their eyes furtively, towards, then away from, the scene. Then came the Captain, who spoke of the evils that men do and how justice needed to be seen to be done. Then the Reverend, dressed all in black, who held out his bible and spoke of God's love, even for those who had lost their way. And then came the hangman – Smith refusing to wear the hood that he offered. And then? It was over. At the drop, the crowd breathed out as one – a collective gasp – that carried the soul of the young man, dancing briefly at the end of the rope, aloft, to join the smoke of the cottage chimneys. And then...where? Several women cried aloud and one, a lover perhaps, fell to the ground and was swiftly carried away. Villain or not, Smith was one of their own – just the latest victim, despatched by a system that did not care. Then the crowd turned its back on the place of execution, and the people started to make their slow way home. It was quiet again; as quiet as the grave.

William and Mac parted ways, each walking homewards, their heads drooped and their hearts heavy. Whatever the justification, a death was a death; a convict's death – after years of clinging to life – a tragedy. William stooped as he entered the cottage, the un-latched door swinging open easily. It took his eyes a moment to adjust, to see the figure of Mary standing silently in the half-light. She was clutching a scrap of paper firmly in her fingers and looked up sharply, as if surprised by the opening of the door.

"Mary? I thought you would still be at Mr Campbell's house."

She ran towards him, and holding him tight, began to sob on his shoulder.

"On account of the hanging..." she explained through her tears, "...Mrs Campbell...let me out early...I came home to fetch my coat...and then –" she struggled to form the words, "found this." Her legs buckled, and as he lowered her to the floor, William eased himself from her arms and took the scrunched-up ball from her hand. Joining her where she sat, with her head pressed hard into her hands, he flattened the paper, and by the weak light of the window made out the scrawled message: *'Wiliam Parker. We now were you liv. Jon Smith was a good freind of us. Be very carful!'* He placed the paper face down, turned to look at Mary, and as though from a great distance, heard her speak again.

"What are we going to do, Will? They know you. They know *me*. Will! We *need* to get away."

William wrapped his arms around her and kissed her hair, leaning on her as much for his own sake as in comfort. He held her as she wept, crying harder than he had ever heard her do before. His eyes scanned the little room as if somewhere, lurking behind the scant furniture perhaps, was an idea, a solution, but none could he find.

"We'll find something, I promise, Mary. We won't let them beat us."

Mary pulled away and dried her face on her sleeve.

"There are *three* of us now," she said, rubbing her stomach with one hand, pointing at William with the other, "Let's hope that we do, William Parker. Let's hope that we do."

The next morning, William and Mary sat together in Campbell's office. He was studying the message the couple had received, when William interrupted his thoughts.

"And then there's this one, Mr Campbell…and this one too," he said, as he slid two more scraps of paper across the top of his boss's desk.

"You didn't tell me about these other two, Will!" Mary looked at him askance.

"I didn't want to alarm you, make you more worried than you already were," he replied, avoiding her eyes. Mary jutted out her bottom lip and kept her silence.

"So, William, how can I help you?" Campbell said, handing the papers back.

"Mr Campbell, have I been a good worker – loyal and diligent in everything you have asked of me?"

Campbell tilted his head, then nodded. "Most certainly. You have shown great aptitude and promise. I have no complaints."

William twisted the hat in his hands. "And you can see that my Mary here is heavy with child. I'm going to be a father."

Campbell nodded again and confirmed that this was plain for anyone to see.

"But I ask you again; how can I help you?"

William looked at Mary then at his boss.

"This place is not safe for us now." His words came tumbling out. "We have enemies on all sides. Smith's friends, as you see, and O'Connor's men too. And Gates, though I have heard nothing of him for months, is still at large. And what, with Mary expecting –"

"Get to the point, William, please."

William took a deep breath. "We need to leave Sydney, Mr Campbell, Sir. We need to leave, and I am asking you to consider a transfer. For me and for Mary. Away from here and those that would have us dead. I know that you have the ear of the Governor and, much as I have valued and enjoyed my time here, Sir, I do implore you to help me in this…" His voice trailed off. He turned to Mary, who squeezed his hand and gave him a small smile.

"You're one of my best men, William and –"

"I realise that, Sir, but –"

Campbell raised a hand and stopped him mid-sentence.

"…and, I was about to say, I will be extremely sad to see you go. But, I do recognise the seriousness of your predicament and would not want to get in the way of you furthering your…" he searched for the word, "advancement, somewhere away from Sydney." He paused then sighed, "The colony at large needs good people like you, William, so, with a heavy heart, I will accede to your request and approach the Governor forthwith. Tell me, how long have you served?"

William sat up and smiled at Mary.

"It's coming up to eleven years, I think, and I do believe that I am eligible for my conditional pardon. Thank you, Mr Campbell, thank you. From both – no, from the three of us."

"And where would you go, or want to go, should the request be granted?"

"To Gregory Blaxland," said William, without hesitation. "He told me that should I ever wish to work for him, he would accept me without question. He is always in need of good stockmen, he said, and as you know I have already met with some of his people."

Campbell rose to his feet and leant forward on his desk, looking at William over the top of his spectacles as he had done on so many occasions.

"My loss will be Gregory's gain, and I know my friend well enough to say that he is sure to honour his promise of a post. I will speak to the Governor tomorrow, first thing, so that you should be ready to leave within the week. You will need to speak to Mac – he will do your job until we find a replacement – and make sure everything is in place for your departure.

The mention of Mac's name made William start.

"Mr Campbell, you will look after Mac, won't you? He's not a young man…"

"Of course, William. It's been good to have you here at the wharf. And now, there is work to be done," he replied.

"Thank you again, Mr Campbell," William replied, the mixed joy of leaving and the concern for his friend muddling his thoughts.

As the pair rose and left the office, Campbell returned to sitting and started to write the letter of recommendation that would change the young couple's lives forever.

Part 2

February 1813

The Emu Plains

18

William stopped and surveyed the scene – the first time he had stopped that day. A flock of several hundred sheep, mostly Merino, also stopped, but their incessant bleating did not. Galvin waved at him from a distant knoll, William replying with a sweep of his hand indicating that that was that: time to call it a day, take a break, then head for home.

A few minutes later, Galvin rode up beside him.

"I thought we'd be here all night, Will. It's been a long day. Time for a bit of tucker?"

"Sure, Sean. Just try stopping me."

The two dismounted and tied up their horses. The heat had subsided but still they instinctively headed for the shade of a tree. Something to lean against. Somewhere to rest your head. William handed his friend a bite, and Galvin reciprocated with a canteen of water.

"Here's to a good day's work my friend." William took a long swig, wiped his mouth on his sleeve, then handed the bottle back.

Neither said much for a while, just lay back against the old gumtree and closed their eyes.

"I remember the first time we met, Will," Galvin said, his eyelids flickering in the low sun. "It was *cattle* that day, some of Mr Blaxland's first, and finest. And then there was that grand old Scottish fellah – Mac."

"Ah, good old Mac," William smiled to himself.

"Any news of him? Is he still alive?"

"The last I heard of him he'd earned his ticket of leave and was growing vegetables on a smallholding, somewhere near Parramatta – away from the fleshpots of Sydney and the worst of the lay-abouts. He was always after the quiet life and deserves a bit of peace for all the years of service to this place."

"Good man, good man," Galvin nodded, then sat up. "And you Will – are you happy with *your* life? You know, here on Mr Blaxland's farm, rounding up *his* sheep, *his* cattle, tending to *his* horses."

William opened his eyes and sat up too.

"*Me?* Me and Mary, do you mean?"

"No Will, just you. Is this life, life working on another man's farm, enough for you?

William leant back again, and thought.

"We had to get out of Sydney, Sean. We feared for our lives, so this place has been..." he searched for the words, "Heaven on Earth compared with what we had. And for Mary and *Billy* – and now for little Lizzie – it's freedom, and space and a dream come true, and...and...so why are you *asking* me this Sean?"

"No reason."

"'No *reason?*' No. There's some reason behind this. If the past few years have taught me anything, it's that Sean Galvin doesn't ask questions for 'no reason'."

Galvin held out the bottle. "Drink, Will?"

"*No*, Sean," he replied, his voice rising, "I want you to tell me what's brought this on. And I'm not budging from under this tree until you do."

Galvin rolled onto his side and started to laugh.

"Sure, you know me too well, William Parker. Right...you know that Mr Blaxland has a long-held notion to find a route into the interior –"

"Beyond the Blue Mountains, do you mean?"

"Precisely. Beyond the Blue Mountains. He's tried twice before and failed. But as you know, he's determined, a man of passion and ambition, and at this very moment he is putting together the final details for another expedition. A new plan, to find a way through."

William nodded quietly, then a moment or two later asked, "And, Sean, how does this involve me? Does it involve *you?* Is *that* what you are telling me?"

"Well, to the second question, the answer is a yes. He wants me to join him, to help look after the horses."

"And to the first?"

"Ah. Now that would all depend on *your* answer, Will."

"My answer? My answer to what?"

Galvin spoke slowly, spelling it out. "To the question of whether you would want to be a part of it, of course." Then he rolled onto his back and stared at the sky. Half a minute later, he turned to face him again.

"Well?"

William also stared, fixing his eyes on the horizon, where the clouds were slowly starting to turn a deep shade of orange. Galvin's question continued to hang in the air.

"I've got a wife, a family...responsibilities...things to think about. We're happy and settled, and –"

"Do you need more time to think about it, Will? Do you need to hear more of what I know? Let's get going and I can explain on the way back."

William nodded, and mounted his horse without another word.

The ride back to the farm was an hour, the horses, tired from a hard day's riding, walking along at a plodding pace. Away from the sheep, the countryside was quiet with only the occasional bark, hoot, or cry disturbing the silence.

"So, tell me again, Sean: Mr Blaxland, Mr Wentworth, and a Lieutenant Lawson to take the lead?"

"Correct. Mr Blaxland sees himself as the one in overall command, but he needs the other gentlemen to lend their assistance. Then there's me, you maybe, and two others – all of us here at His Majesty's pleasure. Oh, and maybe a native guide. That's yet to be decided."

"How long would we – *they* – be away?"

Galvin allowed himself a wry smile.

"*We* – that is, those of us on the expedition – will be away for about three weeks, I think. A day or two shorter perhaps, maybe a bit longer. As nobody has done it before, who's to say?"

"And by which route?"

"Avoiding the valleys. Gaining height, then using the ridges to push a way through the mountains. That's the idea, anyway. Mr Blaxland hasn't told me everything, you know. I'm only a stockman."

The horses walked on slowly.

"So, why me, when there are plenty of others he could have picked?"

"Only the good Lord Himself could answer that one William! Many a time I have asked myself the self-same question: 'Why on earth pick an eejit like Parker when there's so many others to choose from?'"

William tried not to laugh. "No, but seriously Sean, why me?"

"Jaysus, Will, because he trusts you. Because he respects you – knows what you can do with a horse. Up there," he said waving in the vague direction of the hills, "one false step and it could be all over – for the horse and for you. For the expedition too, maybe. You're the only man who can do this. Just *you*, Will."

"And, he asked you to ask me?"

"Correct again. Just think of it, a chance to make your name – not *William Parker, convict* but *William Parker, explorer, discoverer of the interior…hero of the colony* even. Your name would go down in history. Something your children will be able to tell *their* children… but he only wants those who want to come, to join him; so, what shall I say?"

William pulled his horse to a halt, stretched over and grabbed for his friend's hand.

"Tell him I'll do it, Sean. I'll do it!" he said, his face lit up by the broadest of smiles.

19

Mary sat, head in hands, her hair hanging like a dark curtain, hiding her face from William. But he knew that she had been crying, and put a reassuring arm around her.

"Mary…" She moved her hands to her face, now cupping her fingers over her eyes. "Mary," he whispered again, "I'll be back soon. You'll see. And when I return, I'll be famous all over New South Wales. By God! they'll know the name of William Parker as far away as Van Diemen's Land, even back in England I'll wager. And when I come back, I'll be a person of importance. An explorer who found new lands – for King and Country, if that's what they want to believe. Mary, I've got to take this opportunity to make something of myself, for you, and for Billy and Lizzie."

"Shh, you'll wake the baby," she said, then turned to look at her husband. William gently brushed a small tear away with the edge of his thumb and Mary, busying herself, gathered her hair into the long dark plait that hung down as far as her waist.

"But it's so dangerous, Will. Territory that only the black fellahs have seen. It's wild and uncharted, so how can you be so sure that you'll return?" She continued to tease her hair into shape, her fingers working feverishly. "Then what would become of Lizzie, Billy and me?"

William went down on his haunches and took both her hands in his.

"You, Billy, and Lizzie, are all that matters to me now. Of my family in England, I know precious little, and I pray that by the grace of God and the love of friends, that they're still alive. They say that no news is good news, but I have had no news for so many years that all my thoughts have to be for my new family, here. You are all I have; all I live for. D'you not understand that Mary?"

"Of course, I do," said Mary, more fire in her voice. "But that's just it, William – *you* are all that *we* have too! You are…our shield and defender. If anything were to happen to you…" the sentence trailed off, amplifying the silence that now separated them.

A faint cry drifted through the dim light of the cottage, and Mary rose to pick up Lizzie, cuddling the baby to her shoulder. William walked to the door and watched the sun setting beyond the far-off hills, bathing them in a red glow that belied their name. *The Blue Mountains* – he whispered it to himself: mysterious, it transported him to places far beyond the confines of the room. And now, he thought, he had the chance to be one of those who would solve the mystery of what lay on the other side, a chance to play a part in an adventure with a prize so great that it could change the colony forever, and drive it beyond the grey-blue barrier. Onwards, and to who knew where?

The next day, William walked the road to Mr Blaxland's grand South Creek home and waited patiently to be called into his office. Presently he was shown in, to see five more men seated – two on upholstered chairs, three on hard-backed seats brought in from other rooms.

"Ah, Parker. Please, take a seat."

William took the only other chair available and joined the rest of the room facing Blaxland as he stood smiling, his hand resting on a large leather-topped desk.

"Now that we are all here, gentlemen, introductions are in order. I know some of you will know each other but others do not. So, if you will permit me?"

One of the two men sitting on the comfortable chairs, a man in his late thirties, nodded his assent, and the proprietor of the house continued.

"This," he said, indicating the nodding man, "is Lieutenant William Lawson, and to his right Mr Charles Wentworth, both of whom will be assisting me in leading our expedition. And this," he said pointing to a grey-haired man dressed in work clothes, "is Samuel Fairs, who has worked for me for the past three or four years, I think. Here are William Parker and Sean Galvin, two of my best horse men, and lastly, John Whittaker, who works for a neighbour of mine." He nodded in the direction of the men, then continued.

"Gentlemen…I bid you *welcome* and I speak with great humility in the face of the project ahead: to-wit, to find a way and establish a route through the Great Dividing Range. Many have tried, and some have perished, in this great venture." He paused. "And I know that I am but a farmer, but I am an *English* farmer, so I understand not the meaning of fear or failure." He smiled again and proceeded to unfurl a roll of parchment, smoothing it flat on the floor.

"Come, gather round, and look at what awaits us, gentlemen."

A large, roughly drawn map, hand-tinted with blues, greens, and browns spread out before them. To the east, the blue vastness of the ocean was clear, even to the untrained eyes of William and Fairs, the creeks and the rivers, with their azure sinuosity, also clearly speaking for themselves. The lettered names of towns stood out, straight and black, so that William, even when viewing them upside-down, could make out Parramatta, Sydney Cove and Port Jackson. Green stood for fields, criss-crossed by brown lines signifying the sparse network of roads and tracks along which the expanding colony was prematurely, inexorably, reaching its natural limits. And there, to the west, lay the great unknown. It was here where all detail stopped: in reality, where men and horses, sheep and wagons stopped, literally, in their tracks. It was a looming slab of grey, a line of mountains that dominated the western limits of the map. It was the colony's natural prison-wall, God-given and seemingly impenetrable. A breach of this would be a gateway to a promised land, much spoken of, even if, as yet, unseen. Not China, perhaps, but a land whose pastures, when opened by men of courage and vision like those now assembled, would unlock the door to a better future for the sons and daughters of the mother country.

William and the others moved in closer, crouching or kneeling to get a better look. Fairs studied the printed words, soundlessly mouthing the names of the places, resisting the urge to trace the letters with his finger.

"We will start from here – South Creek." Blaxland indicated the place, a tiny agglomeration of dark rectangles. "The horses and dogs I will provide, as well as Nanbaree, a native guide I know and trust."

"A *native* guide?" It was Lawson who broke the silence. "Is that wise, Gregory? How do you know we can trust him? The savages have already attacked settlers up and down the colony, from Port Jackson to Van Diemen's Land. They have destroyed buildings, killed and maimed, men, women, and even children, stolen sheep and cattle…" He looked around him for support.

"As I have *just* said, Lieutenant, I know him. I trust him." Blaxland, avuncular, addressed him patiently. "He has been known to me for the last three years and has even managed to learn some of our language. He is a hard worker and has, I believe, knowledge of the very terrain into which we shall be venturing. It is impossible to be sure, of course, as his language is limited, but we will need all the help we can get, and this is what I, as the leader of the expedition, have decided is the best course of action. Does anyone wish to demure?"

No one commented further. William looked around the group and noted Fairs and Whittaker glancing at each other, sharing perhaps some of Lawson's anxiety, but choosing at that juncture to keep it to themselves.

"I estimate that the journey will take between fourteen and twenty-one days, but we will take enough provisions for a month. We will take this route, avoiding the valleys and keeping to the high ridges." His pointer traced a rough line westwards, from the comforting cluster of farm buildings, each tiny rectangle a reminder of what they would leave behind – all this, and the security it implied, for two or three weeks; maybe more.

Another voice, that of Wentworth, broke in. A tall, bullish man in his early twenties, he spoke with the air of a man who would make his mark in this, the world's youngest country, and one who *would* have his say, whatever the unwritten laws of seniority might be. He stood up, and looked around the room.

"Gregory, since my return from England I have learnt enough to know that a faint heart never achieved anything of any consequence here. We are the leaders, the risk-takers and we must, like Moses, lead our people on, to the Promised Land, unseen and far beyond the horizon. We will, I doubt not, be aided by our good friends here, and on the question of the natives I am in full agreement. Naturally, we have to keep an eye on them but they are a resource like anything else. They are the ones with the very knowledge we need. Good God, man, they can survive in the bush for weeks and months, where a white man would perish in a day. We have got to learn to live with them, use their native cunning, or we may as well resign ourselves to a future confined to what we now see from our bedroom windows. So, tell me," he said, rapping the end of his cane sharply on the bare wooden floorboards, "when do we leave?"

Blaxland smiled and held up the pointer in a gentle rebuke.

"Thank you, but enough of that for later, Charles. Now, would anyone care for a drink?"

William and Fairs, Whittaker and Galvin, joined their more illustrious companions in a glass of rum – rum unlike any they were accustomed to. They raised their glasses, toasted themselves, then toasted The King, and over the next hour talked of nothing but the plans. Lawson studied the map, attending to every detail, questioning Blaxland continuously about his previous expedition into the mountains, offering his own insights into the wisdom of starting with this ridge and avoiding that valley, expounding his theories on what may lie beyond, and showing his expert knowledge of horses and the limits of what they could endure. William kept his own counsel but listened intently, drinking in the leaders' every word.

Fairs and Whittaker also spoke little, save to indicate that they understood what the others were saying. William noticed as their eyes flitted rapidly back and fore, from speaker to map and back again, in their efforts to memorise the plan. This was not a forum to which any of them was accustomed, and after years of servitude each one was, it seemed, desperate to prove their worth in this most ambitious of projects.

Galvin joined William at the edge of the group and raised his second glass of rum. "So, it looks as if we will be leaving soon. Within the week, I wager. Any regrets, Will?"

"No, Sean, no regrets. It seems that we are in good hands. I just pray that we return safely – to our friends and families.

After two hours of talk, maps, and rum, Blaxland finally brought the meeting to a close. Only then did William become aware of the pounding in his chest, the dryness in his throat. This was a moment unlike any other. Success promised security, fame – riches perhaps? Things would never be the same for him or his family. But what of failure, and what this could mean? A return to the toil of his present life, at best. Death at worst.

A final toast – to the Great Divide – marked the end of the proceedings, and William soon found himself making the long walk home, his head abuzz, with dreams of mountains, streams, and the promise of pastures new.

20

Day 1 ~ 11th May 1813

William woke early. That night, he had not slept and had got up in the dark to check, just one more time, that he had packed all that he needed for the journey. Most of what was required would be provided, but personal items were each man's responsibility. By the flickering light of a candle, William unpacked, then re-packed: his horseman's knife, his pipe, his razor, his leather bottle, and a pair of socks that Mary had knitted herself – "my contribution to the expedition," as she'd put it. Being careful not to wake her or the children, he applied one last layer of polish to his old boots, then slipped into his bag a lock of hair that Mary had presented him with the day before.

As daylight seeped into the room, Mary had woken up and he'd promised her again that he would take care and that he would be back soon. Then he'd kissed her on the lips, gently tousled Billy's hair, and laid the back of his hand on the baby's cheek, before unlatching the door and walking into the early-morning chill.

Savouring every step, he made along the track to Blaxland's residence, pausing only when a large female kangaroo sprang across his path, clearing the road easily in one huge bound. It stopped to look enquiringly at the man kicking up the dust, chewed a little, then made its way towards the cover of rough bush a few hundred yards further on. Very different to the pheasants and foxes that would break cover and dart away when, as a young boy, he walked the leafy lanes of Hertfordshire with his father.

All around him was evidence of a wilderness bending to the taming hand of man. Newly erected fences marked out farming plots into squares and rectangles, geometric shapes formerly unseen in the long history of this ancient land. Poles and posts, barns and outbuildings, workers' huts and owners' mansions stood stark against a skyline that had been, until the arrival of the white man, broken only by the motley outlines of eucalyptus and other giants of the bush. But this was a harsh and unforgiving land which demanded respect from poor and rich alike. Out here, and in the mountains to come, Blaxland and his men would occupy the same narrow ledge of existence, a step to either side of which would lead to an early death. Starvation, unquenchable thirst, sunstroke, the bite of the copper-head or the sting of the scorpion, all led to the same inevitable oblivion – regardless of a man's present standing or the fineness of the crib in which he had been laid as a babe.

When Blaxland's farmstead came into view, William jumped the stile to walk the final half-mile of track to the main house itself. He could hear shouting and clearly see small figures carrying bags and bundles from the buildings towards a number of horses standing outside. There were three, maybe four, and the sight of the animals caused his heart to race, injecting an extra spring into his already eager step. It was these horses that would carry them through the mountains, and he, William Parker, was the one entrusted with the responsibility for keeping them fit and well, able to bear the burden of the expedition.

"Ahoy, there!"

It was Blaxland who spotted him first. William raised his hand in salute and hurried to meet him.

The scene now became clear. Four horses stood patiently, nosebags keeping them happy. Nearby, and scattered around, were the sealskin bags and other paraphernalia needed for the journey, with men picking their way between the piles in an atmosphere of organised chaos. Dust filled the air as Blaxland's dogs darted to and fro, barking excitedly at the newcomer.

Blaxland negotiated the maze of bags to greet William, shaking him by the hand and informing him that he was the second to arrive, Galvin already there. In contrast to the meeting some weeks earlier, Blaxland was dressed informally and in a fashion that was almost indistinguishable from that adopted by William and the other men who were now scurrying about, sweating. Today, he wore his shirt sleeves rolled up to just below the elbow, his collar open and tie-less. The trousers he wore showed signs of previous wear and the boots, though polished, were battered and scuffed: a favourite pair. His choice of garments spoke clearly of his intention to get his hands dirty, to be a full and active participant in an expedition that was, after all, his baby.

"Put your bag by that pile, William, and go and help Galvin prepare the horses. He's around here somewhere. The others should be along presently, and when they arrive, we'll have a confab – on the ground, just over there. There'll be no more drawing-rooms for a week or two, and we might as well start as we mean to continue. So, I'll leave you and do what I need to do," he said, before disappearing back into the house. William went over to the animals, laid his hand on the grey, and breathed in deeply.

"William – good to see you on this beautiful morning." A grinning Galvin was coming round the corner. "Are you set? Good. So, these are the beasts that'll be carrying us westwards. As you can see, we've two of our own and two on loan, from Mr Wentworth. *Trigger* and *Ulysses*, you already know," he said, giving each a pat. "And I see you've met *Topper*. She'll go all day and do anything for a handful of oats, won't you girl? This one though…" he shook his head and smiled, "he's got more than a bit of Brumby in him. A bit of a wild boy, aren't you *Copper*?" As he stroked its mane, the horse drew away and looked at him sideward, its eyes large and nervous. "Got to keep an eye on him – a bit on edge, and easily spooked, I'm informed."

"You and me both, *Copper,*" William whispered, and laid his hand gently on its neck. "I like the bad boys, Sean. I'll take this one."

"All yours, my friend. But we need to check them over again before we get going, and you're the man for that job," said Galvin, who folded his arms and stood aside.

William started his inspection of the horses. *Topper* was first. Like *Trigger* and *Ulysses,* she had the look of a pony. Bit of Welsh Mountain, maybe a touch of Connemara. William took a step back, carefully running his eyes over the head and body, noting the ears that pricked at its name, and the large, dark eyes, glancing momentarily towards the sound of his voice. He took in the short, strong neck and the slope of the shoulders then squatted to study the horse's chest: the ribs barely visible – a good sign. Then he made his way carefully around the legs, gently lifting each hoof in turn, looking for damage or the tell-tale signs of disease.

"She's in good fettle, Sean. Got a bit of meat on her, and her hooves are fine. Been well looked after."

William repeated the operation with *Ulysses* and then moved on to *Trigger* who was stamping his foot and breathing hard.

Sean stepped over and ran his hand down the length of the mane, ruffling it as he did so.

"Just showing a bit of independence, a bit of the old spirit, but he'll come round," William observed.

Then they came to *Copper,* an entirely appropriate name, his deep brown coat singling him out further from the others. The Brumbies seemed to have a touch of the gypsy in them. They were dark, wild, and were happiest living as one of the mob; a feral life, going where the rain, the wind or some unseen hand took them, saddles, bridles and reins anathema to their wild, free spirits. This, more than any horse, would have been "broken" – to tame it in the service of man.

While Galvin stayed back, William approached slowly, sidling up to *Copper,* avoiding any contact between its eyes and his own. The

horse neighed softly and stepped away, acknowledging his presence, communicating the first hint of nerves. He stopped, whistled
gently and breathed its name. The horse's ears turned and it tilted
its head, slightly, before returning to look stolidly ahead. He repeated the name and again the horse offered a grudging acknowledgement of his presence. Progress, he thought, progress. One of
Blaxland's dogs that had greeted him earlier found him again and
began sniffing and barking quietly at the newcomer's boots. William shooed him away gently, anxious to keep *Copper* calm; the
horse, however, stood dully, unperturbed by the dogs' antics, the
slight raising of a back hoof the only hint of anything amiss.
Another good sign: the horse was used to the hurly-burly of the
farmyard, clearly inured to the darting and yapping of working
dogs. William waited for the dog's departure before continuing.
Gently saying the horse's name, he stretched out a hand and laid it
with feather-light pressure just above the withers. A shiver ran
across the back, from head to rump, and a shake of the heavy head
told William that *Copper* was finally talking back: *I know you're there.
You're part of my world.* William remained still, his breathing just
audible, the whispering of its name making the animal's ears turn
again, its head nodding imperceptibly. To an onlooker, nothing had
transpired, but to William, these were the next parts of the conversation. This was *Copper's Ahoy!* His *Welcome aboard.* What happened
next would make or break their fledgling relationship. His hand
stayed where it lay, the pressure increasing gradually over the next
few minutes. He repeated its name ten, twenty, times. Slowly, he
started to move his hand down the horse's back, stroking gently,
soothing away the anxiety, continuing to whisper his name.
Through his hand, William felt the strong muscles of the back
tense and relax until the horse finally turned its head to look
directly at whom, or what, had been standing so close.

"G'day *Copper*, nice to meet you," he said unselfconsciously: the
conversation had begun. "Right, my friend, let's see what else you
like."

With his spare hand, he touched the horse's face just above the
muzzle. *Copper* blew from his nose and gave a quiet whinny, but

stood calmly, accepting this next step in the burgeoning relationship.

"Whoa, *Copper.* Everything's going to be just fine," William continued, and the horse seemed to nod its agreement.

William felt the moment had arrived when *Copper* would allow him to take a closer look at his legs and hooves. Continuing to talk, he slowly stroked, then gently lifted, a front leg. A rock in the horse's stance told William that *Copper* was not entirely at ease, but further soothing words, and firm but gentle handling of the hoof, allowed him to make the inspection he knew he had to: for the good of the horse, for the good of the men who depended upon his expertise. As before, the hoof looked to be in reasonable condition, and *Copper* was not showing any difficulty in standing or putting weight on his legs or feet. The real test, however, would be when *Copper* was walking, especially as the ground over which they would be travelling was likely to be rocky and rough, the paths, where they existed at all, long and steep.

Ten minutes later, the examination complete, William ruffled *Copper*'s mane and made his excuses. "Good boy, *Copper.* It's good to make your acquaintance. We'll leave you to enjoy your breakfast in peace." As they moved away, the horse tossed his head and gave another whinny – an equine thank-you.

Just then, Blaxland appeared from behind the wagon and walked over to William and Galvin, beaming.

"Well, young William, *there's* something of a revelation."

"I beg your pardon Mr Blaxland. I don't understand."

"*Copper!* I've not seen anybody yet who could get so close to *Copper* without a fight. According to Lieutenant Lawson, nobody's been able to look at his hooves without at least two other men to help, almost always with the use of ropes and the whip."

William shook his head. "I don't know why, but I've just got a way, Mr Blaxland. Always been able to talk to horses – calm them down so they're not frightened. My father used to say it was a gift, but I think it's just treating them how you would want people to treat you if you were nervous or scared. I don't believe in hurting them – and it just doesn't work."

"Well," said Blaxland, "whatever it is, it's very welcome. Now, the others are due any minute. Whittaker has arrived and is helping Fairs and my men load the wagon. Both of you, come over when you've finished."

In a parody of the meeting held weeks earlier, the circle of men sat on a rough piece of ground, the long shadow of Blaxland's mansion affording them welcome shade from the strengthening sun. A servant brought out water and a bowl of fruit from which their host instructed them to help themselves. The atmosphere was convivial and relaxed as the men swapped stories of what had transpired since their last meeting – of their last-minute prepara-tions and, above all, of their hopes and fears for the adventure to come. Finally, Blaxland called a start to the meeting proper, laid out the map again, weighing it down in each corner. A couple of stones, a glass jug, and a book that William took to be a journal or diary, kept it in place.

"Well, here we are again gentlemen. Welcome to South Creek. The weather, as you can see, is benign this morning, and I expect us to make a start shortly after midday. The horses have been looked over by Mr Parker, and appear to be in good health. Am I not right in this, William?"

William noted Blaxland's use of his first name, cleared his throat and leant up on his elbow. "I've had a quick look and all four seem to be in excellent condition. Testimony to Mr Blaxland, Lieutenant Lawson, and their men, I'd say."

"None of my doing, I'm bound to say, but I've got a good bunch of men here at the farm, so thank you. Please continue."

"Right – the three greys are easy. Very relaxed. But the Brumby –"

"*Part* Brumby," Lawson corrected.

"…yes, he's a bit on the jumpy side. Nothing to be alarmed at, but something to bear in mind on the trail. But I reckon *Copper* and I will make fine travelling companions."

The others laughed and Blaxland assumed control once again.

"Very well. This is where we are now, and here," he circled the tip of his pointer vaguely over an area of mountains in the north-west of the map, "is where we are heading. If I could be more precise, there would be no need for the expedition, but from what I know of the area from previous sojourns, I'd say I'm about right. At the start we will have the luxury of the small wagon over there, but about here," he said, tapping the map, "the path climbs steeply and all our provisions will need to be carried, by our four-footed friends and by each and every one of us – including me. Let me make it clear from the start that the success, or failure, of our venture will depend on one thing and one thing only: teamwork. Yes, I *am* the leader, but I believe that in the wilderness one's rank or station in life mean little, and the further from so-called civilisation we get, the less important our titles become. We will all bleed if cut, all thirst for lack of water, and all rejoice in the beauty of God's creation. In short, we are all but men. And for this reason, I propose that we suspend the usual formalities and call our fellow adventurers by their Christian names, apart from the lieutenant whose title we shall continue to use, in order to distinguish him from William here – unless, of course, anyone vehemently opposes such a *radical* proposition."

He waited, and was about to continue when Wentworth spoke.

"And what of our native guide, Gregory? When is he expected?"

"Ah, Nanbaree, of course. At this very moment he has gone 'walkabout' but Mr Flannery, his master, assures me he will be here by noon. The time, as told by our clocks, means very little to him and his kin, but he can read the sun and stars better than any one of us here. When he arrives, I will make sure he is looked after and understands his role exactly. He will feel quite at home out there, and where our knowledge begins to fade, his will come to the fore. We need to treat him well – whatever our differences."

"Does any one of us have knowledge of his language? Or can we suppose that he speaks The King's English?" Whittaker said, smirking. Somebody else supressed a chuckle.

Blaxland held up his palm for silence, and said seriously, "As I have said before, he knows a little English, and I myself have learned a little of the Dharug's native tongue. Not enough to converse perhaps, but enough I think to make my purpose clear. I have in my saddlebag a copy of Mr Dawes's excellent discourse on the language. It is true that the notebooks were written some time ago, when the colony first started, and that they record only the words and phrases used by the natives of Port Jackson, but I have no doubt that enough similarities exist to make it a most useful text to take with us. Does anyone else have any knowledge of the man's language?"

A number admitted to knowing a few words but none could claim to be confident in its use.

"Very well; has anyone any questions that they feel they would like to ask prior to us making final preparations?" Blaxland surveyed the group with a stern, but fatherly, demeanour. "Remember, that once we have started on our journey, there will be little opportunity to put right what has been overlooked, and apart from what we are able to kill or collect for ourselves, nothing more to sustain us than what we carry through yonder gates."

This prompted some further discussion as to the nature of the rations they would be carrying, the probable scarcity of grass for the horses, and the necessity of making sure all weapons were in good working order. Blaxland then declared the meeting closed and asked every man to make himself useful, however he felt able, in helping to load the wagon and prepare the horses. The group dispersed and William volunteered to help Blaxland's servants load up *Copper*, making his way to where the horses were waiting patiently for their day to begin.

At that moment, and unseen by the men busying themselves with the work in hand, the small figure of Nanbaree walked the last hundred yards towards the house. Of his age no one, including Nanbaree, was sure; and no one, himself included, cared. He walked bare-foot through the dusty approach. He moved lightly, with a languorous, unhurried gait; a contrast to the urgent movements of the men he was soon to join. His clothes, ill-fitting and stained, hung about a body not yet accustomed to the white-man's apparel, but he wore his straw hat, with its wide brim and dangling corks, with an air of practical pride: he, like the visitors to his land, detested the flies. He walked until he stood, unnoticed, a mere fifty feet from the others – it was as if he were invisible, part of the ancient landscape from which he had just emerged. Silently, he observed the men as they hurried, shouting their orders, dropping and recovering objects that he recognised as the tools of the newcomers: pots, pans, shovels and picks. He smiled, chuckling, as they scurried about, sweating and out of breath. So different to his life and that of his own people: these were strange, comical beings from beyond the sea – but they were unpredictable; and dangerous too.

William was the first to notice his arrival and watched him, as he watched them, for a few moments.

"Mr Blaxland," he shouted, pointing to where the guide was standing silently. Blaxland, anxious not to alarm him, slipped off quietly and made his way to the waiting figure.

"Nanbaree. Welcome." Blaxland extended his hand and Nanbaree shook it – a hearty, awkward shake.

"Good day Mr Blaxland," Nanbaree replied flatly, and took off his hat, a sign of respect he had learned from the newcomers.

"Come, please," said Blaxland, and gently ushered him towards the scene that Nanbaree had been quietly surveying.

The ground was now almost clear and the wagon and horses loaded high with the expedition's resources. Whittaker, carrying one last bag, stumbled and fell, the contents spewing itself onto the hard earth, causing the horses to rear and whinny in fright. At this, Nanbaree broke into great laughter, his head thrown back and his body doubled up with mirth. Whittaker, kneeling, met this with undisguised hostility. Slapping a dusty hat onto his thigh and walking towards the newcomer, "What's so funny, *boy*?" he shouted, before Blaxland was able to step between the two and calm the situation. This, observed the expedition leader, was not the start he would have wanted, and hurried Nanbaree to the spot where the group had met earlier, offering him water to drink and fruit to eat. Nanbaree sat easily, cross-legged, on the ground, replaced his own hat and accepted the refreshments he'd been offered, while Whit-taker, still affronted, resumed his task.

Half an hour later, they were ready to leave.

21

Days 1 & 2

It was mid-afternoon when the house, and a posse of waving servants, finally vanished from view. Blaxland led the way on *Ulysses* whilst Lawson and the others followed on foot. The air was clear and bright, and spirits high. William, Galvin, and their horses brought up the rear, chatting as they walked.

"Billy's going to be proud of his da, that's for sure," said Galvin, "and little Lizzie too."

"Well, let's hope you're right, Sean. How did you sleep last night?"

"Not a wink. And yourself?"

"The same. Far too excited. Before I knew it, the sun was up and I was kissing Mary goodbye."

"Not goodbye; *bon voyage*."

"Yes, *bon voyage*."

Galvin kicked out at a dog running through the legs of his horse. "Get away with yeh, yeh wee cur!"

"Not just us who are excited, eh Sean? It must be catching," William laughed.

The party rounded a bluff, and Blaxland raised his hand to speak, bringing them to a halt. Then he dismounted and pointed ahead.

"We'll ford the Nepean just here, traverse the island, then walk to the foot of the ridge that you can just see in the distance. It feels like a long day already, so we'll make camp early, and try to get a good night's sleep. I think we'll all need it."

The group moved on, waded through the shallow waters, then made their way across Emu Island, fording the river again, to reach the far, western, bank of the Nepean. From there on they made good progress, the rich pastureland rising gently as they made for the foot of the ridge. At just before five, they stopped, Blaxland choosing a sheltered, wooded spot where they should set up camp for the night. Whilst the others busied themselves with the tents and fire, William and Galvin saw to the horses. The grass was good and a clear stream provided for men and animals alike.

"He's a clever one, yer man, Lawson." Galvin pointed a hoofpick to where the lieutenant was scribbling in his journal, looking up occasionally to sight his compass on this or that feature. Carefully lined up around him were his instruments: rulers, pens, protractor, compasses.

William carried on brushing *Copper*'s flank. "And thank God for that, Sean. He's the one who'll be bringing us back – hopefully. Look at what we face."

Galvin shielded his eyes and looked up at the ridges towering above them. A mixture of thick forest and scrubby bush formed a patchwork of cover, but the rough terrain – steep rocky gullies, and tracts of scree – was clear to see.

"The horses'll struggle, do you not think, Will?"

William nodded. "Well, it won't be easy, and it will have to be a long, slow haul. But Mr Wentworth is a horse man too, so he'll know what they are, and are not, capable of."

"Gentlemen." Blaxland interrupted their conversation and waved at them to come together. "It's time to eat."

The men sat around the campfire, some on the ground, others on small collapsible stools, each issued with a ration of mutton, dried beef, and damper.

"All from my own animals," Blaxland declared proudly, indicating the food, "but before we eat, I am going to call upon Lieutenant Lawson here to say grace."

Lawson stood up and closed his eyes. He held a small prayer book.

"Dear God, as we embark upon this most noble of undertakings we pray, most humbly, for thy guidance and protection. May we succeed where others have not, and thrive where they failed to prosper. We beseech thee to bless this first of many meals, and ask that thy bounty nourish and sustain us over the coming hours and days. We ask this in the name of thy only son, Jesus Christ, Our Lord; Amen."

"Amen," the group answered together.

William opened his eyes, his attention caught by the sound of Whittaker, his hands still joined in supplication, continuing to pray quietly long after the others had finished and were starting to eat.

When they had finished, they sat around and chatted, a ration of grog loosening tongues and helping the conviviality. Blaxland maintained his position as camp leader, whilst Wentworth held forth on the importance of respecting the colony's convict stock, then entertained them with tales of riding a winner at the Sydney, Hyde Park, races.

"Enough, Charles!" Blaxland laughed, stopping him as he started yet another yarn. "It's getting dark and it's time for us to retire. So, gentlemen, please secure the horses and make sure all equipment is safely stowed away. We'll give the dogs freedom to roam – in case of any unwanted visitors. Till tomorrow then, I'll bid you good night."

A chorus of goodnights followed him to his tent, and one by one, the rest of the company left the warmth of the fire and went to bed. William soon followed suit, and as the birds of the forest finally fell silent, he rested his head on a saddlebag, closed his eyes, and went to sleep.

The following morning, William woke first. His body was stiff, his throat dry.

"Sean. Are you awake?"

Galvin stirred and groaned.

"I am. And I don't care much for the accommodation."

"I'll be back in a minute. I'll get the water on," William said, and left the tent.

He relieved himself, then came back, setting a fire and filling the billy with fresh water. He sat on a stump and watched, mesmerised by the bubbles rising in the pan.

"I thought you were making the tea?" Galvin brought him back to the moment.

"I was. I am. Just faraway."

"Another fair morning, Will," Galvin observed, "and once the dew's lifted it'll be grand weather for walking."

Blaxland was the next one up and joined them for a mug of tea, the others following quickly. Soon, they had all breakfasted, had struck the tents, and were ready to depart. William paused as he overheard Blaxland and Lawson discussing the route, the latter indicating the line they should take, directly up the centre of the main ridge.

"Will, Sean, would you join us, please?"

The two left the horses to join Blaxland and Lawson, who were peering intently at the ridge above them.

Blaxland pointed. "The horses…will they cope with the slope, do you think?"

William looked at Galvin, then back to the party-leader.

"In my opinion, yes. They're tough and used to rough terrain, and they've had an easy time of it so far. As long as we share the load when the going gets too steep or rocky, I don't think it should be a problem. Sean?"

Galvin nodded.

"Well, time we set off then," said Blaxland, patted William on the shoulder, then left to collect his bag.

Once the party were ready, they moved off at a steady pace, *Copper* and *Trigger* leading the way. William and Galvin spoke little, save to discuss the best, and the worst, ways up the spine of the ridge ahead of them, only stopping to briefly rest the horses. The remainder of the men and animals followed slowly, stretched out over a hundred yards or more. Around them, the dogs darted and yapped, chasing each other and anything else that dared to move in the surrounding undergrowth, whilst high in the trees, koalas, solitary and nonchalant, watched them walk by but all the time kept on chewing.

The path, more a vague idea suggested by thinning scrub and smoother ground, stretched out above them. The horses lived up to William's expectations, taking each yard as it came, one carefully-placed hoof following another. As the camp below shrank, then finally disappeared, the animals' exertions became visible in the gleam of sweat on their withers, and in the small clouds that enveloped their muzzles, only to melt into nothingness again. The men too, burdened with provisions for the coming weeks, felt their legs and lungs burn, doubling over to catch their breath, leaning on the larger rocks. And so, they gained height, till far below them the flat plains of Cumberland County, with its scattered farmsteads, and its rivers gleaming in the morning sunshine, presented itself to anyone looking back. Eventually, they assembled above a shoulder where the rake of the initial ascent gave way to a stretch of level ground. Wentworth brought his horse to the front and spoke to William.

"Quite a sight, eh? And half of it mine or Gregory's."

William shook his head and gazed into the distance. Beyond the pasture and the forest lay Sydney, the white sails of its windmills just visible; and then the great blue barrier of the sea.

"And who'd have thought we were running out of grazing land?" William answered.

"That's right, but by Jove we are."

"By Jove!"

They looked round to see a grinning Nanbaree standing nearby, leaning on his spear.

"By Jove!" he said again, then walked away, chuckling.

"He's a strange cove, that one," said Wentworth, "but I wouldn't want to do this without him…so, the worst bit's behind us, eh, William?"

"Well, it could have been worse. We're all here, and the horses seem to be coping with the slope."

"Even this one," Wentworth interjected, ruffling *Copper*'s mane. "So; onwards and upwards?"

"Onwards and upwards, Charles," William smiled, and started walking again.

★ ★ ★

The site chosen for the night was at the head of a deep gulley. The horses were tired and their coats spiked by small pieces of twig collected in the long stretches of thick woodland along the ridge's crest. Whilst the horses were groomed, and the camp set up, Whittaker and Fairs went in search of water, to return, grumbling, an hour later, staggering back up the slope, weighed down by their loads. The horses drank first, the men second, each man receiving a ration of half a pint.

At the end of their meal Blaxland rose and spoke. "Well done, men. The lieutenant tells me that despite the hard going we covered nearly three and a half miles today. I suggest another early night," he declared simply, and no one demurred. The horses fed from a small patch of grass, then the camp fell silent.

22

Days 3-5

Following a good breakfast, the first hour's walking took them higher still, and further west, until the wide-open plains were now a memory, lost behind waves of giant sandstone ridges, and broad, steep-sided valleys, their floors mantled with the blues and greens of eucalyptus. Thick forests, the timber good in places, shaded them from the noonday sun, but also slowed their progress. They plodded on.

"Blaxland. Come!" Nanbaree was standing, at a point where the forest thinned, jabbing his digging stick towards the trunk of a large tree. Blaxland hurried over, his face bathed in sweat.

"Look!"

Hatchet marks cut deep into the bark, at a height slightly above that of a man, clearly indicated that they were not the first to visit the spot.

"Black fellahs?" Blaxland asked. Nanbaree shook his head and pointed towards the rest of the men. "No. *Duggeri-gai, duggeri-gai.*"

"So, Europeans." Blaxland turned and shouted to the others who were now arriving, "Someone has been here before us, gentlemen. They left their mark there, high on the tree."

"Natives or white men?" Wentworth shouted back.

"Europeans. The marks are clearly made with a metal blade of some sort."

A brief frisson of excitement ran through the group.

"Well, at least we must be going along the right lines," somebody commented.

"But they didn't make it," added another.

Sometime later, another mark was spotted, then another. Then nothing.

At various locations along the way, other evidence pointed to the fact that, isolated as they felt, they were not entirely alone: simple bark huts, recently abandoned, and wraiths of blue smoke rising from the valleys below, indicated the presence of native people; unseen eyes that were likely watching their every step. Sharing the wilderness too, were myriad others, four-footed and feathered, that rarely appeared but declared their proximity in the hoots and howls of the night, and in the tattered remains of their departed kin.

As the day wore on, the party was forced on several occasions to retrace their steps. William slowed down and spoke quietly to Galvin.

"We're going to need another meeting, Sean – to tell Blaxland. We just *can't* keep walking the horses blindly onto ridges, only to walk them back again an hour later – when it all ends in a cliff and doesn't lead anywhere."

"You're right Will. Will you tell him, or shall I?"

"I'll do it."

Ten minutes later, Blaxland called the party to a stop at a grassy clearing and invited them to sit in a circle.

"We're going to have to think again about how we proceed, gentlemen. It will not have escaped your notice that we are hardly any further along than we were this morning, and that many of our efforts have come to naught. Will, I think you would like to say something on this."

William stood up and addressed the group.

"It's just that we seem to be wasting time walking blindly in the wrong direction. We walk for an hour only to return the same way. Because of the trees, we can't see where the ridges lead, and more than once the horses have slipped, shedding their loads. It's dangerous, and the horses are getting tired and thirsty."

Wentworth stood up and spoke. "And not just the horses, Gregory. But us two-footed beasts of burden, too." Then turning to Lawson, "What do your calculations tell you? Are we heading the right way?"

Wentworth and William sat down, allowing Lawson to take centre stage.

"It's difficult to be sure. We need to be heading west or west by north-west – and that, by my calculations, is precisely what we have been doing. But we cannot know where a ridge will lead. The forest prevents us from seeing this, so we are forced, as you put it, to walk blindly, and hope for the best."

Blaxland continued, "Thank you, Lieutenant. Well, we appear to have a problem here and cannot spend our time, to all intents and purposes, going round in circles-"

"Could I make a suggestion?" It was Galvin who interjected. "Why not follow the example of our predecessors; the ones who left their marks upon the trees? Why don't we stop soon for the night, then tomorrow, rest the horses while some of us explore the ridges, clear a path, and mark our routes on the trees before returning to camp? We could then take the decision about which route seemed the most promising, and we could proceed the next day knowing that we would not finish the day staring over a cliff."

Blaxland looked to Wentworth and Lawson, who both nodded their agreement.

"Seems like some of the horses' good sense is rubbing off on their guardians," said Wentworth dryly. "I agree with Sean."

Blaxland looked around the group and asked if anyone had any further comments or questions.

"Very well, as nobody has anything to add, I suggest we stop here for the night and follow the plan put forward by Sean. Tomorrow, you and Will can stay behind and see to the horses whilst we reconnoitre the surroundings. We shall know by the end of the day whether or not the plan has been successful."

The next day, the men separated, two groups exploring the surrounding forests, clearing paths and leaving their marks on the trees, while William and Galvin gave the horses a day's rest and checked them over for any signs of injury. And as the sounds of shouting and the hacking of branches faded into the forest, a relative peace descended upon the camp broken only by the chatter of budgerigars and the occasional call of creatures, unseen.

"Will, you never told me the full story. What brought you here?"

"Here?"

"Not *here*. To New South Wales, I mean."

William stopped grooming *Copper* and turned to his friend.

"How much do you want to know, Sean? We all have our secrets."

"Whatever you want to tell me." Galvin shrugged, "I know you arrived – what, ten or eleven years ago…so…did you *kill* someone?"

William resumed the grooming, carefully teasing out a twist of twig that had lodged itself in the horse's mane. Then he paused, the brush brought to his side. For a moment, he said nothing, lost in his own thoughts, then explained:

"We had a fight. He attacked me on the bank of the canal. We fell in and carried on, fighting in the water. It was freezing. I managed to swim to the side, but when I looked back, *he* wasn't there. I dived down, tried to get him out, but he was stuck. A root or something around his ankle. And then…well, it was too late. He was gone."

Galvin waited before asking, "And…who was *he*? And why did he attack you?"

William gave a deep sigh then brushed again.

"Adam. Son of Mr Clarke, the canal owner. My boss. Adam just hated me."

"*Jaysus*…that's not good." Galvin searched for his next words. "So…they got you? Sent you for trial?"

"Hertford Assizes. I didn't stand a chance, Sean – me, a nobody, against the Clarkes. I was going to swing."

"But you didn't. You're still here. So, what happened?"

William shook his head in disbelief.

"Saunders – the Clarkes' butler – he'd seen it all. He was a good man. He stopped the trial – just shouted out from the gallery, told them what he'd seen! The judge had the black cap in his hand, then put it down again – changed it from hanging to fourteen years transportation. I was a dead man come back to life."

"Like Lazarus, in the bible."

"Yes, like Lazarus." He let the thought linger, then turned to face Galvin. "And what about you Sean? What's your story?"

"Ach, nothing so exciting, Will. Theft. I stole a bloody coat – and it was bloody – from a fellow Irishman, killed in the tunnel we were digging out. The sides fell in and crushed him – he didn't stand a chance. But he had no further use for his coat…and I was cold…so I took it. Some bastard reported me to the overseer who I'd crossed on too many occasions. So, before you could say *Jack Robinson,* the authorities were feeling my collar and I was on a ship, Sydney bound. And here we are Will, explorers – loyal servants to The Crown."

William laughed.

"Come on Sean, let's have a nice cup of tea. Isn't that what we English always say at times like this? Your turn to make it."

By six o'clock the camp had reassembled. During the afternoon the two groups had joined forces, having blazed a trail along the same portion of what they now believed to be the main ridge. The men lay about the camp, exhausted, and were slow to come together around the fire. Fairs was the last, complaining that he was feeling ill and had developed a fever. Blaxland cleared his throat.

"Gentlemen, before we eat, we need to reflect upon the day – a very hard day for us all. We need to explain to Will and Sean what transpired, and then we can eat and get some rest. Lieutenant Lawson, how far did we get today?"

"Well," said Lawson consulting his notes, "by my calculations – I normally use two miles an hour as a guide, but today, with all the cutting required, we were a little slower – I believe we were about five miles from here when we turned around."

"Five miles? Very good. And still bearing west?"

"Yes, as far as I am able to calculate this, we are heading in the right direction. As we all saw, we had the main river on our left and the other on our right, the deep gullies we had to traverse, emptying into these valleys."

William raised his hand.

"And the going, what was it like? For horses, I mean."

Blaxland nodded to Lawson that he should continue.

"Not easy, but not impossible. The brushwood is thick, but most of it is weak and breaks away easily with an axe. But the ground is much the same as we have encountered thus far, so we need to remain cautious. Gregory?"

"I have no more to add," said Blaxland, "So let us partake of this repast. Tomorrow we will continue in the same vein. Lieutenant, please lead us in saying grace. And afterwards, could you see what you can find in your medicine chest to help John get over his fever?"

Lawson agreed, and the men ate greedily of their long-awaited meal.

The following morning, straight after breakfast, the camp emptied again, leaving Whittaker, and Fairs, whose fever had worsened, behind with the horses. Using the marks cut into the trees to guide them, the men made their way to the point, five miles distant, where they continued to hack their way along the ridge. Having extended the trail by another two miles they stopped and turned for home, the threat of falling light against them. William and Galvin walked together.

"Not much in the way of food for the horses, Will."

"No. It's just as well that they have had two days' rest. We'll have to see what we can carry of the grass near camp. They won't survive on dust."

On their return, Blaxland sought out Whittaker and Fairs who were together in their tent. Fairs lay, wrapped in a sheet, perspiration beading on his brow. One hand clutched at his bedding while the other hung loosely and shielded his eyes from the light. He seemed to be muttering to himself.

"Still not good, John?"

"No, Gregory. I've made sure he's taken all the powders you said, but his condition has deteriorated since this morning. He'll sometimes sit up and look around, then slump back down and drift into sleep."

"Has he eaten? Or drunk anything?"

"Not much. Just the odd drop of water. But I can't get much sense from him. As you can see, the fever's still on him."

Blaxland knelt down and laid the back of his hand on Fairs' forehead, then stood again and nodded.

"Best leave him for the night. Can you keep an eye on him, John?"

"Of course, Gregory. I'm no physician, but I will pray for his recovery and would ask you to do the same." Blaxland smiled gently then retired to write his journal.

Meanwhile, the remaining men ate their meal and went to bed early. Tomorrow, Sunday, was to be a day of rest.

23

Day 6

It was late in the morning when the first man emerged from his tent. Slowly, hearing the crackle of burning tinder and the hiss of the billy starting to boil, the others appeared until the makeshift seats around the fire were filled with yawning men.

"That blasted emu…calling, all night long! If I could have got my gun, I would have blown it to kingdom come. *And* it would have made a change from the beef." The men remained quiet. Wentworth looked around the group, astonished. "Did you not *hear* it?"

"You would have to be stone deaf, Charles, not to have heard it," said Blaxland, "and every time I dropped off…"

"And then the bloody dogs would start up…"

"Well, at least the grass is soft, and today's a day of rest," Galvin interjected with a smile. "Praise the Lord!"

"Praise the Lord, indeed," said Whittaker, and went back to his bible.

"Is the water boiled yet? I'll make us all a nice cup of tea," Galvin said, casting William a sly look.

Blaxland spoke again. "How's Samuel this morning?" he asked Whittaker, who looked up from what he was reading.

"A little better, I think. He drank some more water and was able to sit for a while, then sank down and went back to sleep."

"Indeed. Thank you, John. Will, could you and I have a word, please?"

William and Blaxland retreated to his tent.

"Gregory?"

"Could you go and find Nanbaree – bring him here. I think we may need to make use of him, to try and get John well enough to walk tomorrow.

Ten minutes later, William returned with Nanbaree in tow. He stood quietly and faced Blaxland.

"Nanbaree. Come with me. To Mr John's tent. John is sick."

Nanbaree nodded and followed Blaxland to where Fairs was half lying, half sitting, surrounded by a clutter of bags and equipment. His eyes fluttered open, then closed again.

"Mr John is hot. Feel his head," said Blaxland, taking the guide's hand and placing his knuckles against Fairs' brow. Fairs gave a lone moan and shivered. Nanbaree said nothing but ran off, returning a few minutes later with a handful of papery bark and leaves.

"Ah, eucalyptus and tea-tree," Blaxland whispered to William.

Kneeling, Nanbaree rubbed the pieces vigorously between his palms to produce a fine litter, the smell of which started to fill the tent. He then held it carefully, cupping it close to Fairs' nose. Fairs opened his eyes wide and instinctively drew back; then relaxed, allowing the vapour to waft around his face. Eventually drifting back into slumber, his breathing appeared easier than it had been for some days. Spotting a shallow bowl, Nanbaree filled it loosely to the brim and laid it next to his fellow adventurer, then raised his hand in salutation and left the tent. Blaxland returned the smile, then left Fairs alone to sleep.

The day at camp was spent, as Galvin had observed, resting. Lawson completed his notes and William and Galvin saw to the horses, whilst the others sat around dozing or making small repairs to their equipment and clothing. Following his visit to Fairs' tent, Nanbaree disappeared once more and would not be seen again until nightfall.

Mid-afternoon, Wentworth found Blaxland half-asleep in his tent, a book open on his lap.

"Gregory. May I have a word?"

Blaxland sat up smartly and stopped the book sliding to the ground. "Of course, Charles. Come in."

Wentworth bent his huge frame and entered the tent.

"Take a seat. How can I help?"

"It's the men, Gregory – especially, as you know, Whittaker and Fairs. They are exhausted, dispirited. Days spent forging on, only to retrace our steps, then push on again, so we are only, what, twelve or thirteen miles from where we started…and then a night without sleep, on account of that infernal bird. It's brought them low – *very* low. And Fairs, you can see he's an ill man, so it's no surprise that Whittaker is questioning the wisdom of carrying on. He's been talking to the others too, to Will and Sean, suggesting, I believe, that we stop and return while we still can. I'm not saying it's a mutiny, Gregory…but I felt you ought to know."

Blaxland closed the book and put it to one side.

"You said, you're not saying it's a mutiny…What *are* you saying?"

Wentworth shifted his position, trying to make himself more comfortable. He lowered his voice.

"They are men first, explorers second. As are we all, Gregory. And, perhaps, they do not share your grand vision. *Our* grand vision," he added quickly.

Blaxland looked up, fixing him with a steady stare.

"And do *you*? Share my grand vision, as you put it?"

Wentworth took out his handkerchief and dabbed at his brow.

"Look, all I am saying is that we need to recognise the limits of what we are capable of. William – Lawson I mean – is a fine surveyor, but here he has so little to go on. It's completely uncharted and with no clear lines of sight. And then there's the threat of natives – we know they are around – and with Fairs ill, Whittaker reading nothing but the Apocalypse, and the horses struggling… Whilst I will do everything to support you –"

Blaxland held up his hand.

"Enough. I'll talk to the men. Later this afternoon."

Wentworth nodded, muttered a "thank you", then left the tent.

"So that, gentlemen, is our position. Is there anything that I have not explained clearly enough? Anything that anyone would like to add?" Blaxland folded his arms and waited. It was Whittaker, sitting next to a blanketed Fairs, who stood up and broke the silence.

"It's the natives, Gregory. How can you be so sure that they mean us no harm? We are pushing farther and farther into their land. We've seen the signs all around us. What do we do if they attack? And where's Nanbaree, now? Is he with them, as we speak?"

Whittaker sat down and Fairs nodded several times, patting him on the back.

Blaxland pointed towards the valley.

"As you know, John, Lieutenant Lawson has made sure we have firearms at the ready, should they be needed. But, as I have said, I do not believe that the natives share the same idea of land as we do. They have no fences, there are no lines drawn upon a map. Yes, they move through the forest, drifting from place to place, hunting or foraging as their instincts take them. But theirs is a simple life – they are *part* of the land and do not 'own' it, as we understand the word. So, what is not seen as *theirs* cannot be taken away by us. And as for Nanbaree, he has no more allegiance to the natives of the forests and hills than he does to us. He is of a different tribe, one of the lowlands people, and as I am sure you are already aware, there's no love lost between the disparate groups." Then he turned to Fairs and, changing the subject, said, "And how are you feeling now, Samuel? You appear to have benefitted from Nanbaree's ministrations."

"I am much improved, thank you, Gregory," he replied, failing to meet his eye.

"Very well; any more questions?"

A murmur, but no more, and the men began to disperse.

"Dinner as usual at six, and an extra ration of rum all round," said Blaxland, then retired to his tent.

The smell of kangaroo meat wafted through the camp. A thick pall of camp-fire smoke rose into the cooling air, and in the shadows the dogs growled and yapped, jealously guarding the scraps of the carcasses which they felt, by all rights, belonged to them alone. Will beat at a pan, calling the men to dinner. Slowly, and with little enthusiasm, they finally assembled.

Wentworth was the first to tuck in. Fairs, sitting at his shoulder, did likewise; first pushing his food around the plate, then eventually eating with more gusto.

"It's not your friend, the emu, Charles, but then it's not beef, either," William quipped. "The dogs have done us proud."

"Never a truer word, Mr Parker. It will make a change. And the extra tot of rum, Gregory?"

"Have no fear, Charles. Here, serve yourself."

Any sense of bonhomie soon evaporated as the camp became quiet again, each man focusing his attention on the plate before him.

"So," said Blaxland, trying to lift the mood, "tomorrow, we shall proceed as we have done for the past two days. We will be rested, and well fed, thanks to Will and Sean. And the horses, Sean? How do you find them?"

"They seem to be fine. No injuries to talk of. Just the odd scratch here and there. And this fodder's good," he added, pulling at a handful of grass, "so we need to load them up with as much as they can carry. We don't know what's up there."

Blaxland smiled benevolently at the group. "That's splendid news. I'd say all is looking fair for an early start," but few returned his smile.

At that moment, a noise caught their attention; the talking stopped abruptly and all looked up to see a dark figure emerging from the forest. It stopped and paused before approaching further.

"Ah! Nanbaree. Welcome back. Is everything all right? All good?"

"All good, Mr Blaxland. Thank you."

"Food? Kangaroo." Blaxland held out his plate.

Nanbaree waved his hand in front of him.

"No. Thank you, Mr Blaxland. I have food," he said, and patted his stomach, then moved away to sit by himself. The men continued to eat in silence.

Whittaker placed his meal on the ground. "Where's he been, Gregory? Do we know? All day, in the forest. What does he do? Whom does he meet?"

"He's his own man, John. He needs to keep moving – the native does not sit and read, or make plans for tomorrow."

"Perhaps he should read this," Whittaker interrupted, holding up his bible, "perhaps it would profit us all if we knew we could trust him; that he was truly one of us."

"John. Nanbaree can never be 'one of us' as you put it," Blaxland replied sharply. "He's a *native*. But I am perfectly satisfied that he is to be trusted and may prove to be invaluable in the days to come. Now, please, eat up, so that we can make final preparations for tomorrow."

While Whittaker and the others finished their meals in near silence, Blaxland moved away and lit up a pipe. Alone, looking up at the starry sky, he slowly became aware of Wentworth standing next to him, also staring upwards.

"Don't worry, Gregory, I'm sure they'll come round," he reassured him, "and even Samuel looks revived. With food in their bellies and a good night's sleep, it'll be different tomorrow. So, I'll bid you goodnight." He clasped a hand on his shoulder. "And let's hope the emu has found some other poor blighters to serenade," he added, more wearily, before disappearing into the darkness.

24

Day 7

The next day dawned cold, and a heavy mist veiled the land. The previous night, no emu had disturbed their sleep, but wild dogs had taken its place, barking and yelping into the small hours. And just as they had quietened, the camp's own dogs had taken up the challenge, accompanied by the grunts, clicks and screeches of anxious possums. Bleary-eyed and fractious, the men struck camp and shouldered their bags. Even the horses seemed to be weary – the lassitude contagious. William and Galvin volunteered to lead for the morning, but the horses, weighed down by the extra loads of grass, moved slowly, encumbered, as they negotiated the steep, narrow paths and pushed their way through stands of dense foliage. The marks, cut into the trees, kept them moving westwards. Finally, they emerged onto an open stretch of ridge; William stopped and pointed towards the valley. "Looks like more natives, Sean – a village, or just a family fire? What do you think?"

Galvin looked to where the smoke lifted and drifted in the gentle breeze.

"Difficult to say with all this mist, although I think there's more than just the one column. Look, there's two, maybe three – they come together."

William peered, trying to make out the scene far below them.

"Perhaps you're right. Whittaker will be reaching for the Holy Book before the end of the day."

Galvin allowed himself a chuckle.

"Well, let's all hope they can speak the King's English. Or his words will be wasted on the wind."

A shout came from below.

"Everything all right?"

"Absolutely, Gregory," Galvin shouted back. "Just admiring the view."

At noon, they rested. The sun was strengthening and slanting through the canopy, the mist starting to evaporate. Blaxland circulated; trying to encourage his party, he spoke to each man individually.

"Ah, Samuel; and how did you sleep?"

Fairs looked up from where he was lying, his hat pulled over his eyes.

"Like everyone else, I assume. If it isn't one animal, it's another."

"Indeed. And John – what about you?"

Whittaker continued to leaf through his bible, his eyes never leaving the page.

"Poorly, Gregory. No respite from the night before. And did you not see the smoke in the valley, as we emerged from the forest? Natives. They are everywhere, Gregory, everywhere. Mark my words. But," he held up the book and fixed him with a stare, "*I* have my protection."

Blaxland smiled, then moved off.

"Jolly good, John, jolly good."

Some four hours later, having travelled a pleasing six or seven miles since breakfast, they decided to stop for the night. The afternoon had been hard going with many, almost insurmountable, obstacles and many changes in direction. Flanking the camp were two deep gullies that dropped steeply to the valley bottom. Blaxland directed William and Galvin to fetch water, and a long time later they returned to the top of the ridge, exhausted by their exertions.

"A tough climb, gentlemen?" Blaxland said, looking down at where they lay on their backs, eyes closed.

William lay, sucking in the air.

"Six hundred feet...straight down...straight up." He angled his hand. "And not much water."

Blaxland looked at the sealskin bag and lifted it easily.

"Enough for the men?"

"Maybe – none for the horses." William fell back and closed his eyes again.

"Very well. Take your time, then join the rest of us. We shall be eating soon."

After dinner, the men sat around as usual, talking over the events of the day. Blaxland, Wentworth, and Lawson wrote in their diaries, the lieutenant adding numbers and drawings to his words. Galvin told stories then stood, silhouetted by the fire, and sang a song – a sad lament for the land of his birth. The others clapped and raised their glasses, before retiring to their tents. William was the last to leave, and was returning from saying goodnight to the horses, when he stopped dead and froze where he stood. By the light of the fire, he imagined he saw a group of men, three at least, standing at the far edge of the camp. He couldn't be sure – then heard a voice. He squatted down, making himself small. The voices continued, whispers only. As his eyes adjusted, he made out the figures more clearly: three natives, one taller than the others. William crept on all fours, searching out the tent he hoped belonged to Nanbaree. In the weak moonlight, it was impossible to be sure.

"Nanbaree! Nanbaree!" he whispered through the material. He heard a movement from inside, then a voice. English. It was Whittaker's.

"What is it Will? What's the matter?"

"Nothing, John. Quiet. I need Nanbaree."

The shuffling continued and he heard Whittaker leaving his tent.

"Will, what's the –"

"Shh! Natives. I need Nanbaree."

Through the darkness, William heard Whittaker move away, mumbling something about the tent opposite, then scrambled the intervening yards, urgently whispering Nanbaree's name. Eventually, Nanbaree's face appeared through the opening.

"Will?"

"Nanbaree, natives. Come quick."

Nanbaree joined William, keeping low, searching the camp for a sight of the visitors. William placed his hand on his shoulder and pointed to the far side of the clearing. Nanbaree nodded, silently.

"Gundungara."

"Mountain people?"

Nanbaree nodded again.

"Good or bad?" William asked. A second or two later came the answer he hoped for: "Good."

At that moment, the silence was shattered by a shout as Whittaker emerged from another part of the camp. Then a second shout – this time the voice was Lawson's. Other voices followed. William turned quickly towards the commotion then broke cover and ran to where Whittaker was closing in on the natives, the bible held aloft in one hand, a rifle in the other.

"John! Put the gun down, John." William ran directly towards him, aiming to cut him off. A movement caught his eye, and in the half-light, William saw the tallest of the native group raise his arm, levelling a spear.

"John, they mean no harm," William screamed as Whittaker stopped, placed his bible down, and reciting the words he knew by heart, took aim. William, throwing himself across the few paces that now separated them, brought him crashing to the earth, and was conscious only of a coruscating flash and an explosion that seemed to fill his head with noise. Lawson arrived immediately afterwards, helping him pin Whittaker to the ground.

"Nanbaree, talk to them. Please!" William shouted and waved him through the smoke that was now starting to clear.

From where he lay, he saw their own native guide slowly approach the group, his hands held at his side. Words were exchanged and the spear lowered. The two others did the same. By the light of the fire, Nanbaree talked, gestured, pointed to the sky. And then, as quickly as they had appeared, the visitors melted away, the white dots and lines adorning their bodies retreating, disappearing, like shooting stars, into the blackness from where they had come.

When William came to, it was to hear the noise of animals and birds, alarmed at the sudden disturbance to their night, accompanied by the sound of whimpering coming from the ground nearby.

"I was trying...trying to *protect* you..." Whittaker was gasping, speaking through his tears, "from men of evil...*from the savage.*"

Blaxland knelt next to Lawson and gripped Whittaker hard by the shoulder. "John, they meant us no harm. And you had no right...*no right* to take the gun. It was not yours to take."

Whittaker suddenly stopped struggling, appeared to regain his composure, and was allowed to sit. Then, on seeing William, he pointed and started shouting once again, "It was him! He is on *their* side – on the side of the heathen."

As the two leaders were forced to tighten their grip again, Blaxland looked to the others and waved them away.

"Go to your beds, men – Lieutenant Lawson and I will deal with this."

William, then Galvin, then Nanbaree and all the others turned for their tents, leaving Whittaker to the care of their betters. The beasts of the forests, and Whittaker himself, fell silent, then William, exhausted, closed his eyes and finally went to sleep.

25

Day 11

The group continued to push further and further west. As the days came and went it was beginning to feel like a treadmill: early-morning starts, the ascents, the inevitable descents, the search for water and fresh grass, worries about natives – and murmurings about the futility of it all. Whittaker, following his late-night discussion with Blaxland and Lawson, kept himself to himself, and for the past two days had immersed himself more and more in his bible; and Fairs looked simply lost.

Early evening, William and Galvin were at the front of the party, which stretched in an untidy line behind them. The days were starting to blend into each other, and William was unsure whether this was the eleventh, or twelfth, but left such details to Lawson. They had made good progress since breakfast, the weather had been favourable and they had kept to the tree line, maintaining good height for much of the day. To the south, they had seen the occasional flash of lightning, followed moments later by the low grumble of thunder, but had taken little notice and plodded on regardless.

"That Whittaker's a strange one, Will. Do you not think?" Galvin said, looking over his shoulder to the group following them up the steep incline.

"Well, he's certainly one for his bible and his praying, if that's what you mean."

"That, and what happened with the natives. Does he not see that without Nanbaree, we would not have got to where we are now?"

William shook his head and smiled.

"And they will have been watching us every step of the way," he said. "We are cutting straight across their territory, and trying to walk unseen…well, it would be like a group of natives walking through the gardens at Government House and hoping nobody notices."

It was Galvin's turn to smile.

"You've hit the nail on the head, Will. If they had wanted to kill us, they could have done it at any time during the past week. The first time we spotted smoke, they would have known we were there. We are sitting ducks," he added, quacked, mimicked hurling a spear at a spot higher up the slope. And then they continued in silence again, each lost in his own private thoughts.

Galvin was the first to be aware, turning to ask, "Can you smell something strange, Will?"

William paused and sniffed the air.

"I'm not sure." He sniffed again. "Smells like…like *burning*!"

He stopped, raised his hand, and shouted to Nanbaree to come over quickly.

"Nanbaree. Smell the air," he said, sniffing for emphasis.

The guide nodded vigorously.

"Fire. Big fire!" he said, and looked round, then pointed at a faint wisp of smoke rising, blue, from deep in the valley. Flocks of birds were starting to gather, wheeling high, filling the sky. Quickly, William handed *Copper*'s reins to Nanbaree, then hurtled down the mountain path to where the rest of the party were lagging, unaware of the threat behind them.

"Gregory!" he shouted, as he ran. "Gregory! There's a fire. Down there!" He gestured wildly in the direction of the valley, where a thin but gathering plume was becoming more plainly visible, rising and billowing above the tops of the trees.

"Fire?" replied Blaxland, unsure, then followed William's finger and saw the smoke for himself.

"We have got to get higher, quickly, Gregory. There's no time to lose. Quick!"

Then he turned and ran as fast as he could, to where Galvin and Nanbaree were waiting with the horses. The others followed quickly, Blaxland's frantic orders and shouts of alarm echoing off the cliffs that towered above them. Exhausted from the run,

William doubled over, felt the burning in his lungs, then straight-ened up and looked all around, trying to appraise the situation. His heart was pounding, his hands beginning to shake. He steadied his breathing and wiped the beads of sweat from his face.

Looking around him, he felt he was in a tunnel, alone: just him, the mountains, and the fire. Nothing else existed. The sound of the others – the shouting and clamour of frightened men, the stamp of horses approaching – melted away as his eyes searched for something, anything, that could protect them. Meanwhile, the narrow plume had become a column, and the smell had now taken on the unmistakable sweetness of burning eucalyptus.

Above, and to their right, William noticed an area of level ground – a small, plateau-like feature, at the foot of a scree-covered slope backed by dark, looming cliffs. Turning, he also noticed that the smoke was drifting slowly away from where he stood. He felt the cool of the breeze on his cheek: the wind was blowing *downhill*. Towards the valley. The plateau, and the breeze: small things, perhaps, but two that might spell the difference between life and death.

He suddenly returned to reality – like a swimmer breaking the surface.

"Gregory. Take the men, up there." He pointed. "Now!"

Blaxland, too bewildered to argue, conveyed this order directly, and the party scrambled towards the lip of the plateau. The horses complained, and as the men staggered and stumbled their way up, their fallen bags littered the mountainside.

"Leave them. Run." William screamed, waving the others past him, to gain height and distance from the approaching conflagra-tion.

Blaxland, struggling to keep up, approached William, who stopped him with a firm arm across the chest.

"Give me the tinderbox, Gregory."

"The tinderbox? Tinderbox? Why on earth do you -"

"The tinderbox! Just give it to me," William repeated, all defer-ence to status and rank, now forgotten – irrelevant.

Confused, Blaxland rummaged in his bag and thrust the box at William, then pushed past and rushed to join the others on the rocky, boulder-strewn shelf.

Only Nanbaree and *Copper* remained.

William stood, clutching the small wooden box to his chest. He closed his eyes, breathed in deeply, then took *Copper*'s reins. Ordered up the hill, Nanbaree started to protest, then ran to join the others. William found the stirrup, and pulling him round, steered *Copper* towards the forest, towards the smoke now starting to blot out the sky. *Copper*, his eyes wide and nostrils flared, reluctantly obeyed his master's command and took them swiftly into the depths of the woods.

"Good boy, *Copper*, keep going," William shouted and pulled him up only when the light was nearly gone, an indication that they were far enough into the trees. The horse slowed suddenly, almost throwing William to the ground, then spun through a half-circle, turning his face to the mountain. At his back, William felt the heat rising and heard the crack of timber and squeal of creatures, the harbingers of the firestorm coming to meet them.

"Good boy, good boy," he whispered, breathlessly, as his trembling fingers struggled to prise open the tinderbox. He fought the urge to cough. What seemed like a lifetime later, the lid came loose and William felt around for the flint, the steel, and the cotton cloth he needed. He knelt and assembled the pieces, spreading the cloth carefully on the ground. He picked up the flint and the steel, steadied his hand, then struck down hard. A spark appeared, briefly, then faded. Again and again, he tried, each time the spark vanishing into thin air; silently, and without trace.

"Come on! Come on!" His eyes welled with tears. He thought of Nanbaree, and how he wished he was there.

"Come *on!*" he finally screamed, desperate, driving the flint down harder still. His eyes widened as a single spark flew, then alighted on the cloth, setting a tiny flame; the smallest of flickers. Immediately, he started to blow, gently coaxing the nascent flame into life, its birth, he prayed, the promise of protection from the finality of death that was inching closer. The edge of the cloth began to smoulder and a discernible fire, miniature, but as real as any other, took hold. *Copper* stamped his hoof and whinnied; William patted his flank, leaning on him as he stood up.

The cloth was now truly alight as William held it to the bark of the nearest eucalyptus. A small flame spluttered into life then skittered its way rapidly up the trunk. William ran to the next tree, then the next, until a row of half a dozen was ablaze. *Copper* was now shying and whinnying loudly, trust in his friend and master evaporating like the sizzling sap of the gumtrees.

"Right *Copper*, let's go." William ran back to the horse, clambering onto his back, digging his heels into his flank.

"Hah!" He encouraged the horse back through the forest, the flames leaping from tree to tree, the crackle of incinerating leaves mixing madly with the bangs and crashing of falling branches. And then, they were out on the open hillside, the suffocation of the forest replaced by air he could actually breathe. William gulped it in, then looking back saw that a front, the length of many houses, was now ablaze, that tongues of flame were licking skywards, purple, blue and red. He dug his heels in harder as *Copper* thundered his way to the stony refuge below the cliffs.

William joined the men hunkering behind their rocky shelters, threw a jacket over the horse's head and crouched, staring wide-eyed at the forest. Nanbaree joined him at his side.

"Big fire, William," he said, shaking his head and breathing fast.

"A very big fire, Nanbaree, very big."

The sound of praying, and not Whittaker's alone, mixed with the terrifying noises coming from just beyond the edge. William saw that the fire he had set now reached the upper limits of the rapidly disappearing tree line, and that the wind blowing from the ridge had pushed the flames away from them – down, to meet the fire below.

Suddenly, and without warning, a huge fireball, every shade of red, yellow and searing white, rolled up from the valley, billowing and churning, high into the evening sky. And then, with a shriek, it collapsed, spreading out towards them, consuming everything it touched. William put his hands to his eyes, shielding them from the heat, and watched in disbelief as the fire-front surged and curled, like the crest of a massive wave, before it finally broke and spilled over, devouring any tree still standing. On it rushed, faster than a horse, until it reached the charred remains of the smaller fire – William's fire…then stopped. Like an angry beast, straining at its chain, it snarled and roared but could not finish the job. It would not chew tonight on the bones of the tiny figures peeping out, a hundred yards away.

The high forest was gone. A smouldering wasteland of charcoal and ashes, there was nothing more for the fire to consume, nothing left to burn.

William let his fingers slip and covered his mouth, too shocked to say anything. It was Nanbaree who spoke for him.

"It finished, Will! It finished!"

The two men laughed and hugged, and cried into each other's shoulders.

"We did it, Nanbaree. We bloody did it," was all he could say before collapsing onto the rocky ground.

That night the party slept badly. Too exhausted and shocked to set up their tents, they slumbered where they sat, using their rescued bags as pillows. In the near distance, the sky glowed red, evidence if they needed it, of the fire's continuing presence deep in the adjacent valley. Then, from nowhere, came thunderous claps, ripping apart the very material of the sky, a sky which emptied in torrents on the men, on the horses, on everything. Hissing steam clouds replaced the smoke, and gradually, so very gradually, the sky turned from red, through orange, to pink and yellow, then eventually to the clear blue-black to which they were accustomed.

It had been a long, hot day.

It would be a long, wet night.

26

Day 19

It had been another trying day, and William was exhausted. Every path seemed to lead nowhere and they had climbed, descended, then climbed again. The ground under their feet was strewn with innumerable loose stones, and the addition of unusually large boulders had made the going almost impossibly tough. During the long hot hours, William found his mind returning to the events of the past days and weeks, and especially to the close encounter with the natives when Whittaker had almost cost them everything. Whittaker – a strange one, as Sean had put it, and getting stranger with every passing mile. Hardly a word had passed between them since Blaxland had waved William away leaving Whittaker staring, mad-eyed, across the forest clearing. But words are not always needed, and every day William felt his hatred. And then there was the fire, and what could have happened to him and the others. And so, his thoughts turned to Mary and his children who could have no inkling how close they had been to losing a loving husband, a doting father. Life was like the path they were following: you walked an endless series of twists and turns, advances and retreats, all the time just a stone's throw from the edge of the precipice.

"Men, we will camp early today. Enough is enough," Blaxland announced. "We need to stop and rest, take stock, and preserve our energies for the exertions of the coming days."

Nobody objected.

He removed his hat and wiped his brow, then indicated the area of flattish ground where the party should pitch their tents for the night. With a collective sigh of relief each man went quietly to his own task. By now, the routines worked like the inside of a well-oiled clock, each man knowing his responsibilities and performing them almost unconsciously. William and Galvin saw to the horses,

Whittaker and Fairs made a start on the tents, while Nanbaree collected what fuel he could find, then busied himself with the fire. Blaxland, Lawson, and Wentworth, meanwhile, found themselves a place to sit, and took out their maps and the other paraphernalia needed to discuss the progress of the expedition, and their plans for the following day. When they had finished their deliberations, they shared a pipe, then lent a hand with the jobs still to be done around the camp; within the hour, it was set up for the night.

Once the horses had been fed and watered, William walked over to where Blaxland and Lawson were sitting. Lawson was working on the map and notes he was compiling – what would, months later, form the record detailing their historic journey.

"Gregory, Lieutenant," William said, taking off his hat.

"Will. It's been a long day. Did you want something?" said Lawson, looking up from his sketch.

"Yes. I feel the need to have a little time to myself, so if I may, I would like to take an hour away from the camp. I'll take *Copper* and won't stray far. I could reconnoitre the area further on, just beyond the trees," he said, pointing. "I won't go far," he repeated, then stood and awaited their reply.

Lawson looked at Blaxland who indicated with a nod that this would be fine, but as William turned to go, Blaxland spoke.

"Are you unwell, Will?"

"No, not unwell Gregory. Just tired and in need of some time to myself – but only by your leave, of course."

"Of course," said Blaxland, "but be sure to return by the time the sun starts to drop. We don't want to lose you over the edge, or, God forbid, to the wild dogs." He gave him a weak smile, then returned to his writing.

Ten minutes later, William was sitting astride *Copper*, a thin column of smoke from Nanbaree's fire marking the camp's position. They walked on a few hundred yards more to a broad, dusty ledge where William pulled back on the reins and gave the horse's neck a gentle slap.

"Right-o boy, let's stop here and rest awhile," he said wearily, then slipped easily off *Copper*'s broad back. He tethered him loosely to a fallen bough lying a few feet from the edge of the cliff, from which they had an uninterrupted view of the lands beyond; stretching, he thought, to the edge of infinity. He rubbed the horse's muzzle before lying down next to the log, making himself as comfortable as he could.

"I gave my word to Lieutenant Lawson that I would report back, and so I will. But first, old fellah," he said, stretching, "a bit of shut-eye." *Copper* blew gently as William lent his head against the papery bark and closed his eyes, allowing his thoughts to return to his own bed, home, and family. The silence enveloped him, and as he settled on the ground the tension in his aching muscles began slowly to subside. Whittaker, the natives, and the fire all seemed a long way away. Before long, he was asleep and snoring quietly.

As his master dozed, *Copper* stood sentinel – happy to be still…

William woke with a start. A prolonged whinny told him that something was not right. An animal? A snake, perhaps? The horse, William knew all too well, was much afraid of snakes and would bolt if one slithered into view. But *Copper* had not bolted and stood, stamping the ground, snorting quietly.

"What is it, boy?" William asked, twisting to look around. Seeing nothing, he closed his eyes again and pulled his hat down. *Copper* continued to shift uneasily, snorting more loudly, and pulling at his tether, until William sat up and looked around again. He stood, his back to the drop, and surveyed the scrub between them and the high ridge, then, in case of snakes, he studied the ground by his feet.

"There's nothing there, *Copper*, just the breeze blowing through the trees."

He patted the horse's flanks, then returned to lying, his hat tipped over his nose.

"Just a few more sec–"

His head jolted backwards and the log, once his pillow, now felt like an instrument of torture. A forearm gripped his throat. Thoughts of Gates, and the attack on Mary, flooded his brain. The grip tightened further and his head began to swim. Struggling for his life, he finally grasped the arm, prised it away, then rolled to the side and scrambled to his feet.

"O ye of little faith! For the Lord will execute judgement *by fire and his sword* on all flesh, and those slain by the Lord will be many."

William held his arms out in front of him and sucked in the air.

"Whittaker? What the hell are you doing? Are you possessed? Put that knife down. For God's sakes man, what is this?"

In his right hand, Whittaker held a large knife. Open, and cradled in his left palm, lay his beloved bible. His eyes blazed, flecks of spittle mottled his beard as he continued to rant, half to William and half, it seemed, to the ether.

"Behold, they have become like stubble. Fire burns them; they cannot deliver themselves from the power of the flame," he continued, his hand shaking, the bible almost falling to the ground.

"Stop!" William screamed as Whittaker began to advance, his wild eyes fixing on his, then searching the sky for something, or someone, in the clouds.

"The natives – I warned you about the natives – warned *all* of you. But *you*, William Parker, *you* would not listen. And then…" he grimaced, his voice at a whisper, "the fire – the fire, Will."

"No. It was not the natives." William shook his head vigorously, "It was a storm, lightning."

Whittaker was inching closer. William stooped and crabbed to the other side of *Copper*, controlling his voice, watching Whittaker's every move. The horse shifted, uneasy.

"Don't do this, the fire was *not* of the black-fellahs' doing. Put your knife down and let us talk. What ails you so, John?"

The use of his first name brought Whittaker momentarily to his senses.

"Ails me? What *ails* me?" He looked astonished. "This," he said, brandishing his bible. "And this," he said more softly, indicating the forest and the valley with a long slow sweep of his arm. William noticed his eyes slowly starting to fill with tears. Then, without warning, he lunged forward, catching *Copper*'s flank with a sharp blow. The horse reared, his forelegs windmilling viciously, out of control. A heavy hoof struck Whittaker between the eyes. He staggered backwards, dropping the knife to the ground, then put his hand to his head and looked down at his fingers, slowly turning crimson. Blood coursed freely from the gash, blinding him as it filled his eyes, streaming down in rills to drench his face and chest. Raising his head, he staggered backwards, amazed, while William struggled desperately to control the shying horse.

"John! The edge!" William screamed, looking up, "Stay away from the edge!" He tried to find a way round *Copper*, by now bucking and straining, pulling dangerously at his tether.

"John!"

But it was too late. With a look of bewilderment, Whittaker stepped back. Glancing just once, uncomprehending, at William and the horse, he disappeared from sight, the only evidence that he had ever existed, a prolonged, fading cry, and the scatter of pages, fluttering down like confetti into the cool, clear air of the canyon.

Too late.

27

Day 20

They stood in a semi-circle: Blaxland, Lawson, Wentworth and William. A dirty, red-brown stain stretched across the ground, starting at the log, ending abruptly at the edge of the cliff. No place left to go. Nearby, a single page fluttered madly in the gusting breeze, pinned to a bush of thorns.

"This is the log," William pointed, "and over there is a page from his bible…" He trailed off, stopped, and stared mutely at the ground.

Blaxland knelt down and scooped up a small handful of dark-brown dust. He held it for Lawson and Wentworth to see – they nodded; then Blaxland slapped his hands clean, returning the dust to the earth.

"I'm sorry Will, we had to be sure."

"I understand, Gregory."

"And *Samuel*," said Lawson, "he confirmed that John had suddenly disappeared, and that the knife they had been using to cut up the meat was nowhere to be seen."

"And then there's the blood on *Copper*'s hoof, *and* the mark on his side," added Wentworth.

"Thank you, Lieutenant, thank you Charles," William said, then stood silently for what would happen next.

Blaxland took off his hat and held it to his chest. The others did the same.

"Lieutenant. Would you say a few words before we leave? It seems the least we should do. Then we will need to descend, and try to find his body; before the dogs do. He deserves a Christian burial."

Lawson stepped forward and closed his eyes. He paused, then asked God to remember His child John, and to welcome him to Paradise. A few lines committed to memory from the very same book that Whittaker had held so dear; then the party was walking slowly back to camp.

They arrived to find the tents down, the horses packed, the fire doused and steaming. Subdued, and quietly going about their business, the men readied themselves for the coming day.

Galvin walked out to meet William, and without a word put his arm around his shoulders and steered him back towards the horses.

Once they were ready to leave, Blaxland came over to William and Galvin.

"There was a ravine, a gulley, about half a mile back. Do you remember it, Sean?"

Galvin thought for a moment and confirmed that he did.

"The one with the small brook? No wider than this?" he said, and held his hands shoulder width apart.

"The very one. Do you think the horses could make their way down?"

"It depends. We couldn't see more than a hundred feet before the land fell away sharply. If we unloaded them, perhaps? Or at least, lessened their burden. I think maybe we could. What do you think, Will?"

William said nothing, but nodded.

"That's settled then," said Blaxland, and told them that they were to take the lead. "Where you go, the others will follow, Will," he added, with a reassuring smile.

When they reached the gulley, they stopped.

"I'll go and look, Sean. You wait here," William said firmly, then headed down, to reappear ten minutes later with the news that as they had believed, the horses could, if relieved of their loads, make it down safely.

"But it will be slow," he said, "and still dangerous. We are about five to six hundred feet above the main valley floor. The gulley's very narrow, and the rocks loose and liable to break away. We all need to be patient, and take it slowly."

"We'll wait for you, Will. You go first; then Sean. The rest of us will follow in good time," Blaxland said, then went to explain to the others what was happening.

William unloaded *Copper's* bags and laid them in a pile at the top — Galvin and the other men followed suit. They had agreed, "horses first, baggage second", as without the horses safely down, the bags themselves would be as good as useless. Once William had gone, the others were to wait for a sign, a whistle, before starting their own way down. A few minutes later, Sean and the others disappeared from view as William led *Copper* into the first part of the descent and felt the vertical sandstone cliffs starting to close in on him.

"Whoa! Take it easy old fellah." William grabbed the reins as the horse threatened to lose his footing on the loose, wet rocks of the gulley floor. His voice echoed wildly, bouncing from one wall to the other several times before fading to nothing. *Copper's* nostrils flared and his eyes widened, telling William in his own way that this particular manoeuvre was stretching their friendship to the limits.

"I know *Copper*, I know," William soothed, rubbing the horse's nose, then stopped a minute before whistling for the others to start their descent.

It was Galvin who came next, the ricocheting voice confirming, several times, that he was on his way, before it too bled into the silence.

William pulled gently at *Copper*'s reins, coaxing him down the next part of the slope. Here, the narrow passage levelled out a little, took a sharp bend, then fell away again steeply. *Copper*'s legs straightened and his head pulled back, resisting, before trusting again in his master so that they were able to lose a few more feet in height. William paused once more, took a breath, then led him down again.

Suddenly, the quiet of the gulley was shattered, first by urgent shouting, then almost immediately by the noise of rocks tumbling down. William turned around just in time to see the first of a slew of boulders hurtling towards them. Bouncing, arcing, somersaulting from above, some the size of his fist, others bigger than his head; each would spell an instant, bloody end. He fell to the ground, hugging his knees, making himself small, while *Copper* reared and struggled to keep his footing. For ever, it seemed, the rocks kept on coming, until the roar, like that of a passing, marauding mob, faded to a distant whisper, silenced only as they reached the valley bottom. *Copper* continued to neigh loudly, rearing and pulling at his rein. It was only then that William came to his senses, threw his arms around the neck of the horse he loved, and spoke quietly into his ear.

Once *Copper* was calm, William stood aside and cupped his hands to his mouth. "Sean. Sean. Stop where you are." His shouts reverberated upwards. "Can you hear me?"

"I can. Are you all right?"

"We're fine, just fine," William lied. "But stay where you are until we reach the bottom. Do you understand, Sean?"

"I do, Will. We're grand where we are. Just tell us when you're ready."

"That's good, Sean – I'll give you a long, loud whistle."

"A loud whistle. I hear you."

Slowly and carefully, William and *Copper* descended, all the time listening for the clatter of falling rocks; but the only sounds they heard were the cawing of ravens and those of *Copper's* hooves. Twenty minutes later, with the horse at a safe distance from the gulley, William put his fingers to his mouth. His whistle, loud and shrill, momentarily filled the valley. And then came the answer: Sean and the rest of the party would be joining them soon.

Blaxland looked around the valley floor, then consulted his watch. The descent had taken longer than expected and it was now two o'clock. Dividing the party into three pairs, he explained his plan.

"We will split up and, in our pairs, spend two hours searching for John's body. Two hours. No longer. Nanbaree will stay in camp and prepare the fire for tonight's meal. I want us all back here by four-thirty, at the latest. Charles and William have watches, and we are all synchronised. If you find the body of our friend, you are to ensure you note exactly where it is, how to find it again, so that we can inter him properly first thing in the morning. We will walk together to the foot of the cliff where I will direct who will go where. Are there any questions? No? Well then, let's get going."

At four fifteen, William and Blaxland returned, dejected. The camp was silent, the fire built, but not set, Nanbaree nowhere to be seen. At four twenty, Wentworth and Galvin appeared and two minutes later Lawson and Fairs. They all had the same sad news: that there was no news. It was then decided, to build a small cairn, to fashion a cross from two branches lashed with twine, and to mark it with a sign, made of bark and written in ink. Lawson was to do the writing. As Fairs, grumbling, got the fire going, William and Galvin gathered the rocks, and Wentworth carefully fashioned the bars of the cross, binding them together tightly. Lawson, meanwhile, had found a suitable piece of bark and carefully wrote the message:

Near Here Lyeth
The Body of
John Whittaker
A Man of God
Died 29th May 1813
RIP

"Nanbaree appears to have gone walkabout again," said Blaxland, looking around.

"Maybe the smell of the cooking will bring him back," Fairs said. "Maybe he'll develop a liking for civilised food," he added, and poked the fire so hard that a large cloud of sparks filled the air.

At that moment, Nanbaree himself appeared from behind a small clump of trees, something dark clasped in his hand.

"There's yer man there," said Galvin, and everybody turned to watch Nanbaree make his slow approach. Heading straight for Blaxland, he held out his hand, and placed the small battered bible on the ground, at his feet.

"Mr John. He near." He pointed in the direction from which he had come, and beckoned to Blaxland and the others to follow him.

That evening, the meal was eaten in silence, each man lost to his thoughts. Nearby, Whittaker lay in a shallow grave topped by a pile of sandstone rocks. The shadow of the cross, meanwhile, moved slowly across the group until the light of the sun finally disappeared from view, and the grey, insubstantial form was itself subsumed by the encroaching dark of the valley. High above, looking like row upon row of dark hanging bags, a huge colony of bats roused itself and lifted noisily into the blue-black sky; then all was quiet again. Once the meal was eaten, the men wandered back to their tents, the only sound, the excited, faraway bark of a wild dog.

28

Day 21 ~ 31st May 1813

Breakfast was a sombre affair. Galvin joined William, and after a minute broke the silence.

"A rough night?"

"A bit."

"I heard you crying out – it must have been in the wee hours."

"I had nightmares, Sean. I kept seeing Whittaker step back, and each time I reached out to grab him, he fell backwards – over and over again. It was as if I'd pushed him."

Galvin drank his tea.

"You can't blame yourself. He wasn't right." He tapped his head. "You know, in *here*. And *he* came looking for you, Will, with a knife. *You* did nothing wrong."

William pushed the food around his plate and let out a deep sigh.

"I know Sean, and you're right. But...it's still hard; hard to understand."

From behind, they heard a strained voice saying, "Samuel, please, you have to eat." It was Blaxland, sitting next to Fairs. The camp was in shock, in mourning.

Galvin tried to change the subject.

"Have you seen Nanbaree this morning, Will?"

"Can't say I have. The fire was already set when I left the tent. He must have gone walkabout again, I suppose."

"That's possible. He must have been spooked by John's death," Galvin said, threw the dregs of his drink away, then stood up. "We'll be moving out soon. I wonder how much longer we can go on like this," he added.

Five miles to the west, Nanbaree stopped and turned to look back. A thin curl of smoke was just visible above the trees. *Ah! breakfast, and their English tea,* he thought, then ate a handful of bunya nuts and carried on running.

By ten o'clock, the party had packed up camp and were heading away from the mountains, crossing flat, open land towards the line of low hills that formed the western horizon. In the distance, a group of kangaroos looked up and eyed them quizzically before bounding off effortlessly, and from their vantage point high over-head, a pair of wedge-tailed eagles soared and swooped, watching the tiny figures edging slowly westwards.

William looked over his shoulder, at the line of horses, dogs, and men following them – their mounting fatigue more obvious with every mile. Blaxland was making an effort to look in control, chatting to Lawson and pointing at things; but then his head would drop, and he would return to a plodding walk, planting one weary foot in front of the other.

Galvin noticed William's stare, and nodded. "Gregory looks all-in Will," he said, making sure his words didn't carry on the breeze. "D'you think this could be it? The end of the dream, I mean. Since John died, he's looked like a changed man, and I'm wondering if he's even thinking straight anymore. Just look at us." He pointed to their clothes, tattered and stained, and the shoes that were falling off their feet, "Give us a day, two at the most, and we'll be going around like Nanbaree's kin, barefoot and half-naked."

William looked grim. "This time, I think you could be right, Sean. He's a natural-born leader – tough and determined, but even he must accept that there has to be an end sometime. It might be that it's now or never."

At midday they stopped, allowing the horses to graze on the better grasses of the lower ground. It was still not good, William noted, but better than anything the mountains had been able to dish up. The men spread out with only William and Sean sitting close to each other. Fairs had moved off to sit by himself, his back towards the group, staring into the waters of a muddy brook. And even Blaxland and the other leaders sat silently apart, seemingly lost in their own private thoughts. Nanbaree had still not reappeared. William and Galvin exchanged knowing looks, but they too ate their lunch in silence. Overhead, the eagles continued to circle.

Barely ten minutes after they stopped, Blaxland announced that they had to be moving on. The men grumbled quietly before they reluctantly forced themselves to stand, ready to resume walking. Fairs appeared not to have heard Blaxland's order first time and had to be reminded loudly to join the group. He walked slowly, head down, keeping his distance. He was, William thought, like a petulant child refusing to catch up with his parents.

By two o'clock, the open plain had closed in around them and they were now approaching the foot of a long, wooded slope, the culmination of which was a low, sugarloaf-shaped summit. Up ahead, Blaxland stopped and waited for the others to join him. The slope was not as steep as the one they had slipped and scrambled down the day before, but a hill is a hill, and every man turned to their leader anxious to know what was on his mind.

He stood and faced them.

"Men," he said, forcing a weak smile, "I realise this journey has been long and hard. I know we are all weary, ready to turn around and head for home. I know that we all – and I include myself – miss our loved ones, the familiarities, the pleasures, the chores even, of everyday life. In short, we are exhausted. And all of us, I am sure, are deeply saddened and shocked by the loss of John, God rest his soul."

He paused. A long pause. The men stood silently, anticipating, the tinkling of a nearby stream the only sound. They stood, caps in hand, awaiting his decision.

"But for what would he have died if we were to turn back now? For nothing, men, for nothing," he said. "And so, we carry on," he concluded with a nod, then turned on his heel and began to climb.

"But Gregory –" someone started to say, then stopped as Blaxland walked away, a stubborn determination in his gait.

Halfway up, the woods grew darker and the temperature dropped rapidly. A heavy silence hung over the party as the men and their animals trudged half-heartedly upwards.

Galvin spoke to William, a quiet aside: "If we push on much further, it's more gravestones that Lawson will be after writing."

The route through the forest followed a dry riverbed, the lofty trees and thick undergrowth blocking out most of the light. Blaxland strode ahead whilst William and *Copper* followed about twenty yards behind, trying to keep up. Below them, Galvin had dropped back and was having difficulty coaxing *Trigger* to move any faster than a slow walk, whilst the rest of the party trailed further down the slope, trudging their way upwards, their eyes focused firmly on their feet. The forest was quiet save for the occasional crash of branches as a startled bird made for the sky, somewhere, unseen, above them.

"One foot in front of the other, old boy." William encouraged the horse over the cobbles and boulders that covered the ground, conscious of his own thighs starting to burn. "It can't be long until we turn around and head for the hills again, then home."

A loud shout, a familiar voice, broke the silence.

"Mr Blaxland!"

William turned around, unsure where to look.

"Mr Blaxland!"

"It's Nanbaree, Will. Up the hill."

William followed Galvin's finger to see Nanbaree running down towards them, his arms flailing excitedly, until he finally came to a sliding halt.

"Nanbaree. What's wrong?" Blaxland said, the worry of recent days clear in his voice.

"Not wrong – *good,* Mr Blaxland. Come. Quickly," said Nanbaree, then turned and started heading back up the slope, followed closely by a rejuvenated Blaxland, now desperate to discover what "good thing" lay ahead.

William slapped *Copper* on the rump, and grabbing his harness led him as fast as they both could go up the incline, further into the forest. Sensing something important, the others began to increase their pace, Lawson and Wentworth urging them onwards.

As the slope started to level, and the forest thinned, William became aware of the burgeoning opalescent light and the fresh, cooling breeze; then, as if someone had pulled back a theatre curtain, he was standing in the open, Blaxland and Nanbaree just feet away. It was like being on stage, or on a ship's deck, amid a sea of greens, browns and yellows. They were standing on a promontory, a rocky platform that seemed to float on air as it jutted out, away from the incarceration of the forest, towards the promised freedoms of the west. All three stood and stared. Silent. Dumbfounded.

Suddenly, the spell was broken, as first Galvin, then the others, arrived and took in what it was they were seeing.

Nanbaree turned to face his audience and beamed. Then with a flourish, he waved his arm. "This my land. Nanbaree's land!" he said, and giving them a broad, toothy smile presented the view for their inspection.

A spontaneous cheer sent more birds flying, then each and every one of the party hugged each other, shook hands, and congratulated themselves on doing what no other settler had succeeded in doing before: finding a route to the west.

Below them, stretching as far as they could see, from left to right, was flat land – a wide grassy plateau punctuated here and there by low, wooded hills, and criss-crossed by rivers, gleaming now in the kind autumn sunlight. Had he been here to see it, this would have been Whittaker's biblical "promised land."

It was Lawson who finally took control and spoke.

"This," he said, pointing towards the vast swathes of land below them, "is the best watered country of *any* I have seen in The Colony."

"And," added Blaxland, his eyes moist with relief, "there's enough forest and grassland before us to support and stock the colony for the next…*thirty* years!" He turned to his men – bedraggled and exhausted – and spoke with a voice that was close to breaking. "Gentlemen, today we have made history. Today, we have achieved what we set out to do, and all our names will go down in the annals of His Majesty's colony. With the greatest of fortitude, and by the grace of the good Lord Jesus Christ, we now stand and look out on what will be, in a matter of just a few years, the breadbasket of our great venture. Today, I thank you and am certain that on our return you will all be amply rewarded, be you free settler or convict. And now, before we turn our backs on all this and return to the forest, I bid you look one last time on this bountiful landscape. Three cheers for King George!"

Then, with the huzzahs ringing in their ears, the party turned around and made their way back through the forest, back to Whittaker's cross, where they set up camp for the night. The dogs, not to be outdone by their masters, were successful too, and caught a joey, allowing the men to eat better than they had for a week. The rum flowed freely so that the pain of their blisters and the aches in their limbs were soon forgotten, and song and laughter reverberated through the valley. They had succeeded in what they had intended to do.

And now, they were going home.

29

Day 27 ~ 6th June 1813

The journey home was uneventful. By the end of the first afternoon, the effects of the previous night's drinking had worn off and the euphoria replaced by a dull torpor borrowed from the days leading up to the final hill. And then they had set off for home, closely retracing the tracks that had led them to their destination; no longer "explorers" now – just weary travellers in need of a hot meal, and a good night's sleep in a bed that they knew. For just under a week, they had dragged themselves eastwards, each morning following the sun, happy to turn to their native guide to ease their aching legs and to soothe the blisters and cuts that hurt more on the inward than on the outward journey. Today, they had descended the ridge; another final hill. William looked down at his feet, now showing through his boots. *Sean was right,* he thought, *barefoot and half-naked.* But at least the countryside was beginning to look more familiar and there were hours, rather than days, to go. This was fortunate, as the men, he could see, were on their last legs, almost literally, with each man feeling the cramps in his belly, each weighed down by the overwhelming shared sense of fatigue.

"I recognise this place," Galvin said to William, his voice no more than a dry croak.

"Me too – thank God," William replied.

"Flat, open land. No need to look for cuts in the bloody trees, Will. I always hated hide and seek."

"Should be home by the afternoon – I heard them talking. Nanbaree's run ahead, to tell them we're nearly there."

Galvin shook his head. "Yer man, Nanbaree. Where would we be without him? Probably at the foot of some ravine," he said, answering his own question.

They plodded on.

The sun was low in the sky when they passed the place where they had camped and eaten together on the first night. The place where Wentworth had entertained them with his stories and where Lawson had prayed for God to guide and protect them, to grant them success in their great venture. His prayers had been answered – apart, of course, from the tragedy of Whittaker's death – one of God's own, whose very ghost seemed to ride alongside them on their return. And now they were nearly home.

William's reverie was broken by a shout.

"They know we are close, gentlemen. They are coming out to meet us!" Blaxland had summoned all his strength and was now striding out, leading his men towards the banks of the river they had once regarded as the unspoken frontier between home and the unknown. As they prepared to ford the Nepean, his shout, like a call to arms, rippled through the party, and every man straightened and stood a little taller: the rag-tag battalion that had dared to take on the untamed wilds of the Blue Mountains was now returning. Battered, bloodied, but victorious.

The first to appear was Elizabeth Blaxland, sitting atop an empty buckboard wagon that had come as far as it was able, to the southern bank of the river. Next to her was a boy, the eldest of Blaxland's seven children. They waved, and Blaxland waved back, the military leader momentarily supplanted by a husband and father.

Slowly, others appeared. Farm workers, servants, a pair of horses. And then Mary.

William felt his throat tighten, tried to keep the tears from coming. He peered, searching, trying to see more clearly, and then he saw them – Billy peeping out from behind his mother's skirts, Lizzie swaddled in her arms. He too waved, and Mary waved back, shyly.

Copper stooped to drink before giving in to the pull of the rein and wading through the water, onto Emu Island, then back into the water again. They were close enough to talk.

"Will, you look a mess. What happened to your head?"

William grinned and ruffled his hair.

"I don't know what to say!"

Mary laughed and rocked the baby in her arms. Billy edged a little closer but stayed latched onto his mother's legs.

Finally, they left the water and William was able to walk the remaining few yards to where his family waited. He put out his arms then looked down at his shirt and trousers.

"I'm filthy," he said.

"Indeed, you are," Mary replied, then hugged him until he felt he could hardly breathe. Lizzie woke and started crying. William planted a soft kiss on his daughter's cheek, and ran his fingers gently through her hair.

"And where's my Billy?" William said, looked all around him, then bent down and picked up his son, hugging him until he pleaded to be let go.

"What's that?" Billy asked, pointing to William's beard, "You don't look like my papa."

Both William and Mary laughed and hugged again.

"Don't worry, Billy. That's him. Papa's home!"

They were sitting at the table, empty plates and dishes, a jug of water, pieces of crust and half-eaten fruit all that was left of the first proper meal William had eaten in almost a month. Lizzie was fast asleep in her crib, and Billy, allowed to stay up to talk with his father, was dozing, with his forehead resting next to his bowl.

"And," said William in a whisper, "Gregory – Mr Blaxland – has said that he would recommend to the Governor that we all get our pardons and a hundred acres of land. A *hundred* acres!"

Mary put her hand to her mouth and gasped, then she stood up and wrapped her arms about his neck.

"My hero. Our hero," she said, then moved away and picked up the baby.

"Time to put these two to bed. Then it's us. I'll do this; you get ready."

Ten minutes passed and William was lying, waiting. He stretched out, luxuriating in the softness and the warmth of the bed, fighting the urge to close his eyes and go to sleep. A candle cast its soft light on the curtain, like that of the full moon.

The door creaked closed and he felt Mary slip in beside him.

"Fast asleep," she said, then reached out and felt for his hand. William took hers in his and pressed her fingers to his mouth.

"I've missed you," he said, kissing each of the tips in turn. "It's good to be home."

Mary laid a finger gently on his lips, silencing him.

"Shh. There will be time enough to talk…tomorrow." She pulled herself in close, then whispered in his ear, "But for now, you can carry on exploring – the hills, the valleys, the secret places…" He felt the warmth of her body next to his, and allowed his hand to search beneath the fabric of her nightdress, roaming the softness of her skin, breathing in her scent. And then she was on top of him, breathing hard, pushing back his hair and pressing her mouth to his. William opened his eyes, briefly, saw the flicker of the flame playing upon the ceiling beyond the blackness of her hair, then closed his eyes again. Suddenly she stopped. Pulled away.

"What is it, Mary? What's wrong?"

"I've just got to tell you something, Will."

William waited, held his breath.

"I love you. I love you, and a hundred acres, or no hundred acres, I always will. Now, William Parker, please make love to me."

William and Galvin were sitting with their heads close together, sharing a joke. They, like the others in the room, were dressed to the nines, hair brushed and beards trimmed. It was six weeks since they had crossed The Nepean for the final time, and the story – *their* story – had rippled through New South Wales like wind through a wheat field. What they had done was the talk of the town, from the bars and barracks of Sydney and Parramatta to the whorehouses of Hobart: overnight the colony had grown in size and the way to the west was waiting. The sound of silver on crystal caused them to look up.

"And now, gentlemen, if I may have your attention. And may I say how smart you all look this afternoon. A damn sight more respectable than the last time we were together!"

Blaxland waited for the laughter to subside before continuing. He held up an envelope, repositioned his spectacles and looked down his nose at the audience. He was milking every moment.

"I suppose you might be wondering what I have in this envelope? Why I have summoned you here today? Surely, not just to share a glass of rum, however convivial."

William shifted in his seat and loosened his collar while Blaxland laboriously searched for his paperknife, carefully slit open the large buff envelope, then extricated the contents, a single sheet of quality paper. He held it at arm's length, studying it before turning to his audience with a smile.

"It's from Governor Macquarie; a letter." He cleared his throat. "And it reads:

My Dear Gregory,
May I be the first to offer my congratulations and heartfelt thanks to you and
your party for what you have done in the service of His Majesty King George

and the Government of New South Wales. In finding a safe and reliable route through the Blue Mountains you have secured the future of the Colony and one can only imagine the trials and tribulations that you and your men must have endured in this heroic venture, an undertaking that embodies the spirit and selfless determination to succeed, upon which, all of our prosperity depends.

As a gesture of appreciation and reward for your courage and fortitude I can confirm the following:

You; Lieutenant William Lawson; and Mr Charles Wentworth shall each receive a land grant of an additional One Thousand acres, the locations to be agreed."

The room turned to the men in question and clapped uproariously, offering their hearty congratulations.

"Former convicts…" Blaxland paused and looked over the top of his spectacles. William turned to Galvin and beamed. *"Former convicts Galvin and Fairs are to be granted their certificates of freedom, Parker an absolute pardon, and each a grant of land equating to Five Hundred Acres per man. This is to be in the vicinity of the area known as The Emu Plains, the exact location yet to be decided. The unfortunate sacrifice made by the late John Whittaker has been duly noted.*

In relation to the naming of the various landmarks encountered along the way, I am pleased to accept the proposal of Mount Blaxland as the final point of the journey, and will confirm the remaining proposals in due course.

Once again, I offer you my congratulations and trust you will convey the enclosed information to each member of your party,

Sincerely,

Major General Lachlan Macquarie,

Governor

New South Wales."

Blaxland placed the letter back in the envelope.

"Gentlemen, you will remember this map," he said, letting drop a linen cloth. "The newly drawn red line marks our route, meticulously calculated by our friend Lieutenant Lawson here, every length and change of direction carefully logged each evening, as you will all no doubt recall. Here, as indicated by Governor Macquarie himself, is the newly named Mount Blaxland. Other geographical features, as yet undecided, will be named to mark Lieutenant Lawson's and Mr Wentworth's invaluable contributions."

Blaxland himself led the resulting applause, then waited for silence.

"And so, my friends, it just leaves me to thank you once again, to congratulate each and every one of you, and to wish you good fortune for the future. Make good the land you have been granted and cherish the new freedoms you now enjoy."

Outside the grand house, William, Galvin, and Fairs assembled, for one last time as "the men who conquered the Blue Mountains". They stood in silence, each holding a document that proclaimed they were now free men.

"And what about Nanbaree? What has become of him, I wonder?" William looked at Galvin and Fairs for an answer, but all he received was a shrugging of shoulders.

"What would he want?" Galvin said. "What could they give that would mean anything to him? A house? A smallholding? Smart clothes? No. None of these things."

Fairs said nothing more and rolled his pardon carefully into the shape of a tube.

Then they shook hands, grasped shoulders, and wished each other the best of luck, before going their separate ways and leaving, in the truest sense of the word, for pastures new.

Part 3

September 1814

The Emu Plains

30

William was standing in the eye of a maelstrom – a whirlpool of animal noise and tumbling confusion. As he watched his sheep arrive, he reflected that even if his flock was by no means the biggest in New South Wales, it was still, he believed, one of the best, and that the money he and Mary had saved from their time in the Campbells' employ had been wisely spent. The Merinos had thick fleeces of the highest quality – white, bright, and soft – and the beasts were of such a size that his younger, childish self would have thought them to be things of pure fantasy – creatures that could only exist in his mother's bedtime tales or as part of his own innocent musings. Earlier that morning, little Billy, more often a hindrance than a help, had whinged and whined until Mary had finally given in and let him jump onto the wagon, allowed him to make the hour-long journey to the shearing sheds. Sitting proudly next to his father, he was sometimes even allowed to take the reins.

From the shade of the veranda, and holding a fractious Lizzie, Mary had waved them off. "For pity's sake, William," she'd shouted after them, "remember he's not yet five – don't allow him to stray! And Billy, stay close to Papa – and make sure he comes home as soon as the shearing's done! And take care on the road…" And then they disappeared into the bush.

As usual, the yards around the shearing sheds were a turmoil of bleating, cursing and banter. Wagons and riders came in from miles around, the horses' hooves and creaking wheels throwing up billowing clouds of orange dust. Billy rubbed his eyes and coughed uncontrollably.

"Cover your face and take a swig of this," William said, and handed his son a bottle. "*You* wanted to come. I told you what it was like."

Billy grimaced. He hid his face in his hat and pulled hard on the water, the cough subsiding slowly.

"Now Billy, we've got to find Gumtree. See if you can spot him before I do." William and his son started to scan the crowd. All around them hundreds of sheep continued to pour in. It felt, he thought, as if there had been a blizzard, a heavy fall of snow blocking the roads and filling the corners of the square.

"There!" Billy shouted excitedly, and pointed at the lumbering form of his father's lead drover, half hidden by an in-coming wagon but still standing a full head and shoulders above the crowd. After much gesticulation and shouting, the three finally met, Gumtree shaking William firmly by the hand and bending low to greet Billy.

"I see you 'ave a new partner today, Mr Parker," he said, his huge hand ruffling the boy's hair. Billy's smile disappeared rapidly as he took refuge behind his father's legs.

"Come back here and stand by my side," said William. "I told you, the shearing's a hectic place, and if you want to be my partner you need to stand straight and tall. The Governor, he doesn't grant land to those who run away every time someone talks to them. You have to show him, Billy, prove to him that you're a man."

Billy slowly left his father's shadow and came to stand next to him again, his eyes fixed sullenly on the drover.

"Right, Gumtree," William said, clapping his hands, "Let's make a start," and the three of them wended their way through the throng, into the sheds where the shearers were preparing themselves for the exertions of the coming day.

As they entered the cool of the sheds, the noise levels seemed to increase tenfold, the bleating and the yelling reverberating off the low timber roof.

"Are we taking them *all* on today?" William shouted.

"Aye, Mr Parker," Gumtree shouted back, "I've got rid of the wasters, and these are all good men – as far as I can tell, of course."

"Well, you've not let me down before," William said, and slapped the drover on the shoulder. "Best get them going – time is money and there's a lot of sheep, over-dressed and waiting for their services."

William and Gumtree had wandered off so Billy stood to one side and watched as the men prepared for the sheep to be let in. To him, it seemed, all the men looked the same, each wearing a large bushy beard, each dressed in a collarless shirt, sleeves rolled up, thick trousers string-tied at the knee, stout boots, and the ubiquitous wide-brimmed hat. Some wore waistcoats or loose jackets; others had hung theirs on pegs around the shed walls. A few chatted whilst they could, as their mates sharpened their shears or took a last swig from their bottles. Outside, the dogs barked, excited, then a bell rang out urgently and the first of the sheep were funnelled in from the holding pens. Billy stepped back as the Merinos were dragged or manhandled past to where they would be shorn – standing almost eye to eye with him, some with spiral horns the size of his head; these were animals to be respected.

Different men, Billy noticed, had different techniques. He noted that some stood and grasped the struggling animal between their knees whilst the man further along wrestled his to the floor and knelt as he worked; the one next to him sat and worked on a low three-legged stool. All clipped away with the same vigorous action, their shearer's forearms the thickness of his leg. The heavy fleeces fell away silently onto the smooth battened floor, the more skilful shearers amongst them managing to produce a single, magnificent coat, the less experienced settling for two or three raggedy pieces. Billy stood mesmerised, the click-clack of the metal shears almost literally cutting through the background din: hooves clattering floorboards, the laughter and cursing of men, the thud of bales as the piles grew high, and the bleating of startled animals. A cacophony to some, maybe, but music to the ears of men whose living depended on it.

Billy wasn't the only boy there that day, but *they* were three years or more older, sons of his father's men, more used than he to the rough and tumble of the sheds. Where Billy kept to the shadows, they swaggered and strutted their way through the crowd of workers and animals, ducking cuffs aimed at their ears, swearing and spitting with the best of the men, as they swept the floor clean, or waddled to the storage pens weighed down by an armful of fleeces. Billy tried to join in but, bumped and jostled, was quick to retreat to the safety of the nearest alcove.

At about midday, Billy's stomach rumbled loudly – it had been an early start and he was already missing his mother's cooking. He sat in a corner while all around him the shearing went on uninterrupted, the men eating their "tucker" and swigging their beers as they worked, with the piles of fleeces getting higher and higher. The smell of the sheep, mixed with the stench of sweat and beer, filled the still air, and Billy began to feel unwell. He aimed for the light of the doorway at the far end of the shed, dodging and weaving his way through a forest of legs, horned heads and mountains of wool. Finally reaching the exit, he stumbled out into the harsh glare of noon, sat on a bench and cried. A minute later he heard a voice.

"What's up mate? Got yerself lost?"

He looked up at a kindly face and nodded. Suddenly he was riding high, perched on the shoulders of a bearded man, looking down at the tops of heads – he ducked as they re-entered the sheds, then made their way towards the office.

William was bent over a large ledger, explaining something to Gumtree, when the door swung open.

"Beggin' your pardon. Found this one, boss – thought he might belong to you." The man lowered Billy gently to the floor.

William looked up and for a second said nothing.

"Bloody h–!" he stopped himself swearing further. "*Where* have you been Billy?"

"Just out there, papa. Where *you* left me." He ran over and buried his face in William's side.

"Thanks, Jake. You can, er, get back to the sheds now."

The man smiled knowingly, touched his hat, and left.

"So, you got lost did you Billy? Easily done. You're not in trouble. No need to let mama know…let's get something to eat, eh?"

William told Gumtree to take a break, then sat with Billy while they ate the food Mary had prepared for them that morning.

For the rest of the day Billy never left his father's side and when the faint light of their cottage window finally came into sight, he was still fast asleep on his father's shoulder.

31

William sat astride *Copper*, the Parker cottage slowly retreating behind him. He rode alone, Mary's words still ringing in his ears.

"She was right, *Copper*. Billy's far too young for Parramatta. Best leave him at home when the market's on."

Copper snorted.

"Glad you agree," he said, and dug his heels gently into the horse's flanks, breaking him into a reluctant canter.

"C'mon old boy, it's not that far."

He and his horse had travelled this way many times before, and as familiar landmarks came and went, he relaxed into the ride. For all its harshness, he had come to love the landscape of his adopted homeland; the rolling green of his Hertfordshire childhood now felt distant and strange, like a picture from someone else's life. Here and there, small stands of eucalyptus and weeping myall – the only trees hardy enough to withstand the frequent drought and fires – interrupted the broad sweep of the skyline; it was an ancient landscape, as yet largely untamed, but one, he knew, that held untold promise for those with the will and energy to succeed.

Halfway to their destination, William slowed as he spotted, rising from behind a low hill, a column of blue smoke. Standing tall and steady, it spiralled slowly upwards before drifting gently sideward to disappear at a height inhabited by eagles alone.

"Could be natives, could be bushrangers," he said to himself. He knew that along with the great promise came the threat of violence: from those who had lost this, their homeland, or from those newcomers who had lost their liberty, *their* home still half a world away. Which would be the worse group to encounter? He pondered the question, but finding no good answer, galloped on, scanning the horizon for any more signs of danger.

As they got nearer to Parramatta, the emptiness of the bush slowly gave way to a scatter of buildings: well-maintained cottages, shepherds' huts, farm-sheds and shacks – the settled, the well-to-do, a stone's throw from those barely hanging on to existence itself. Such was life in the colony. Other travellers, also bound for market, started to appear – many on horseback or driving wagons, but some simply footslogging their way along the dusty roads, steering themselves towards the centre of town. The herds of cattle and flocks of sheep descending on the town were a clear indication of the week's main event, but many others came simply to enjoy the fairground atmosphere, to meet old friends, and to eat; and some, to drink themselves into a stupor: sometimes, people need to forget, he thought.

William's route brought him to the bridge, crossing the river close to the government farm. All around, gangs of convicts, flanked by ever-present guards, toiled away at the labours he remembered only too well from his old life, in Sydney. One or two looked up as he passed, but mostly they did not, too lost in their own thoughts and their hard, humdrum lives. He trotted on to the foot of The Crescent, the low hill from which Government House looked down and from where it kept a baleful eye on the town and its people. William stopped and looked up at Governor Macquarie's residence – it had grown since his last visit. The convicts had been hard at it: two new wings, and a splendid portico, held up by two pairs of ornate columns, gave the house the appearance of a grand English home, reminding him of the time he and his father had first visited the Clarkes' residence in Hensford, when he was still just a boy. He allowed his thoughts to drift to the chain of events that led to Adam Clarke's death; and then to his arrest and eventual transport to New South Wales. He shuddered and turned *Copper* towards the High Street, a wide thoroughfare lined by houses and other fine buildings. In a few minutes, they came to a stop at the front of The Mason's Arms where he was to spend the night. By the entrance to the inn, a set of stocks, wide enough to accommodate three unfortunate people, reminded William that the rule of law, of sorts at least, was still in place. He remembered his own time strapped to the flogger's triangle, shuddered again, and walked inside.

The room was dark, and a number of traders and their men were already drinking hard. He peered into the gloom and waved at the man behind the bar.

"Mr Parker. Good to see you, mate!" The publican came from behind the counter, wiped his hand on his apron and shook him firmly by the hand.

"Good to see you too, John. Business booming?" said William, nodding towards the drinkers.

"Always busy when the market's on. Tonight, it'll be standing room only in here," he replied with a smile.

"Usual room, John? The one at the back."

"Too right, mate. It's quiet – well, as quiet as it gets here, if you follow my drift."

"I do, and if I may, I'll leave you my bag, John, and get straight into town. Is that all right? Oh, and *Copper's* outside. Will you see he gets fed and watered?"

"Not a problem, boss. Have a good day."

William handed over his bag and left, kissing his horse on the nose as he passed.

Heading for the market, he wove his way through the mass of people thronging the streets, many crowding around the dozens of stalls and stands that dominated the town each May. Now in its tenth year, the market continued to grow, drawing in the crowds from across the ever-expanding colony – pastoralists, merchants, ladies of the night…they all made rich pickings at the annual fair.

He had arranged to meet Gumtree and the men at the market place, a short distance from the river and only a few minutes stroll from The Mason's. They had made their own way down the previous day, their lumbering carts piled high with the Merino fleeces destined for the spinning-towns of Leeds, Halifax, and Bradford. Gumtree was not hard to spot, and he and William were soon chatting, leaning against the wagons under which he and the half-dozen others had slept the previous night.

"Did you get much shut-eye, my friend?" William enquired.

"Not much, not with this lot and Rushton's Brewery within staggering distance," he replied, and jerked his thumb at the group of men now sleeping it off in the shade of the wool packs. "But I kept a clear head, boss. Plenty of larrikins wandering around the place only too happy to have a barney and make off with some of the merchandise."

William laughed. "You're a good man to have around, Gumtree. Now let's get this stuff off the wagons and into market. The sale starts at noon."

Two hours later, they were jostling for space in the centre of the floor. The men had gone, told to "disappear, and have some fun – no questions asked."

The hammer came down on lot 36.

"Ours next," said William, and nodded at the stack of bales nearby.

"I'd stop your nodding, Will," said Gumtree, "or you'll be buying your own stuff back."

The bidding started quickly with William and Gumtree straining to follow as the bids came in from all around the crowded floor; then, as the price topped 40 cents a pound, things started to slow with four, then three, then just two men still in. But the bids continued to come in, "42…43…do I hear 44 cents? No? So, at 43 cents…going once, going twice," the hammer came down with a crack, "gone, to Mr Jackson for *43 cents* a pound!"

Amid the excitement, William hugged Gumtree and repeated the price; then the voice of the auctioneer cut through the hubbub: "From what I remember of the Yorkshire winters, they're going to be needing their woollens."

"Never mind the winters, what about the bloody summers?" replied a wag.

"Let's go," William shouted above the laughter, and the two made their way through the crowd, the air hanging thick with the smell of stale sweat and tobacco.

Towards the back of the room, someone grabbed William's shoulder. "Great price, cobber, best I can remember!" he said.

"A great price, indeed – and one that needs celebrating," Gumtree agreed, then steered William towards the nearest bar.

By the early evening, the inns and drinking dens were chock-full. The beer was flowing, mostly down the throats of men, eager to quench their thirsts, but the floors too were awash with Rushton's Best. A fog of pipe smoke completed the picture.

William, Gumtree, and their gang were competing for space in the front bar of the Mason's Arms, the noise of the crowd going up as the beer went down. Groups of workers, some friendly, others not, banded together, swapping tales of the day – losses, gains, the easiness, or otherwise, of the local women – each man had his story.

"Give the men some room," William said, close to Gumtree's ear, and gestured that they should move to a far corner of the bar. "They need to say what they like about us – we've driven them hard these past few days," he mouthed clearly.

Gumtree nodded to show he had heard, and the pair elbowed their way through the crowd to find a place by the door, the start of a dark passage leading to the yard at the back of the building.

"So, Gumtree, a good day's work?" William said, now just able to make himself heard.

"Absolutely, boss. A good price for good wool. Once again, it stood out from the rest. Something we can be proud of."

William smiled, raised his glass and clinked it against Gumtree's bottle.

"Upwards and onwards!"

"Upwards and onwards!" his friend agreed and took a long draught of beer.

Suddenly, the broad smile fell from William's face, his eyes settling on a point at the far end of the room.

"Problem, Will?" Gumtree asked, and turned to scan the crowd.

"Could be. Someone I'd rather you didn't meet. And he's coming this way."

Moments later, he stood before them, a little unsteady, the beer spilling from his jar soaking the already wet sawdust floor. The beard was thicker and shaggier than William recalled, hiding the scar on his cheek. But the eyes, thought William, were the same cold jellies he remembered so well from Sydney. Cold, cruel, calculating. How could he ever forget them?

"Well, well, well! If it isn't me ol' mucker Will-ee-am Parker!" he said, spitting out the name a few inches from William's face. "Who would have fuckin' believed it?"

He rocked back onto his heels and took a noisy swig of beer.

"Will?" Gumtree said, looking confused.

"Gumtree, this is Gates – Tommy Gates," said William, breathing hard. "I had the misfortune to know him in Sydney."

"And I, the *good* fortune to know the lovely Mary – just a little better," leered Gates. "Oh, and by the by, William," he said, leaning in closer and reducing his voice to a whisper, "there's something *else* I know…something *you* should know that *I* know…"

William waited in silence.

"Very well," said Gates straightening up, "I know you murdered Adam Clarke. He of *High Trees*. Mr Clarke and my good father are associates – more maybe? Cobbers, mates, as your sort might call them." He took another swig and spat it at William's feet. "The Parker name, it stinks of shit in Hensford – no! – across the whole fuckin' county."

William squared up to him, "Just get out Tommy, if you know what's good for you."

Gates looked over to where his friends were laughing and joshing, unaware of his departure.

"D'you hear that, mates?" he shouted. "If – I – know – wha's good f'me!" he said, slurring, though no one *could* hear him over the noise of the bar. He smiled a stupid grin, then swung out with all his force, the wide arc of his fist catching William full on the mouth.

William staggered backwards, knocking into several drinkers before finding himself holding a handful of sawdust, staring at a forest of boots. For a second, the world seemed to go deathly quiet, and he felt all eyes turn to watch him, rubbing his chin, getting to his feet, standing again, unsteady.

Then everything went crazy.

The first thing he was aware of was Gates spiralling to the floor, his jacket filthy, now covered in blood, then a stool flying across the space that was rapidly forming in the centre of the crowd. He saw Gumtree fend off the piece of furniture, then lift off his feet and toss to the side someone foolish enough to try and follow up the chair with a kick. From another corner, he heard someone shouting "Gumtree! Will!" followed by a string of expletives and a surge in the room which made him duck and hold up his fists, in defence of what he was sure was to come. A bottle smashed, then another, and a pair of men entered the fray, one pushing and grabbing at the other's hair, the pair crashing to the floor in an explosion of screams, stale beer and sawdust. William's head spun and his mouth started to hurt as more and more men were sucked in to the mass of bodies milling and flailing in front of him. Another bottle smashed against the back of the bar, followed a second later by the crash of glass as the mirror hit the floor. More shouts, more screams, Gates flat on his back, vomit mixing with the blood and beer in his beard. William backed away, his eyes darting from left to right and back again, trying to make sense of a scene that defied description. Friends and foes were now all as one, one blood-splattered face much the same as the next, arms, legs and flying objects all adding to the scene of utter confusion. Then something hit his head and his knees buckled, putting him again close to the floor. The room was spinning, and he thought he was about to fall, when he felt his legs go from beneath him, heard the din of the fight receding, and the dark of a cool passage closing in. Suddenly, it was light again, and he was on his back looking up at the sky, Gumtree standing over him, breathing heavily, his huge hands upon his hips.

"Shit, boss, that was some commotion! But your friend Tommy – he won't remember much of it!"

William closed his eyes and allowed himself a little laugh.

"Friend? No friend of mine, Gumtree. What just happened?" He rubbed his chin and winced.

Gumtree said nothing and held out his hand, hauling William to his feet.

"Fancy a beer?"

Inside, the sound of breaking glass and shouting indicated that the fight was still going on and would likely last a while longer yet.

"Not really thirsty, mate," William grinned. "To tell the truth, I think I've had enough of the market today. When it's all died down, I'll sneak in the back, grab my bag and get home to Mary. Take care, Gumtree. Get yourself down to the Red Cow if you're still thirsty. Better class of customer, I believe. I'll see you back at the farm."

With that, Gumtree tipped his hat and made his way around the side of the inn, towards the High Street, leaving William to figure out a way of retrieving his bag without being seen.

True to form, *Copper* had plodded his way home, unconcerned at the darkness that had descended an hour into the journey. It had been an uneventful trip, especially when compared with what had transpired a few hours earlier, and William had enjoyed the peace, the solitude and the steady clip-clop of his favourite companion.

The beer and the excitement of the day made him drowsy and he was surprised when he woke to find himself outside the door of the cottage.

The faint light from a window indicated that Mary was still awake, surprising William as it was late and she had not expected him home that night.

He opened the door quietly, to find Mary sitting at the table, head in her hands, apparently dozing. She looked up, shocked at his arrival. He covered his swollen lip with his hand.

"Mary? What's the matter? Have you been crying?" He threw down his bag and rushed over, placing his hands on her shoulders. "Mary?"

She pulled herself free from his embrace, holding a letter out towards him. He noticed that her hand was shaking.

"Oh, William, I am so sorry. I had to read it."

William first noticed the broken seal, then the black line running around the edge of the letter. He took the paper and opened it slowly, scared and mystified in equal measure.

Squinting in the weak light of the oil lamp, he suddenly stopped.

"It's from my mother," he said blankly.

32

William sat down heavily and smoothed the paper onto the table-top. The room was dark, so Mary moved the lamp towards him, a pool of pale-yellow light illuminating the neat copperplate script. William muttered a thankyou then started to read, silently to him-self.

"Please Will, read it aloud so that I can hear," Mary said, softly, placing her hand on his forearm.

Regaining his composure, he sat up and read:

Hensford, England, September 1814.

"That's over six months ago, Mary."

My Dearest William,

I hope, by the grace of God, that this letter finds you well. As you know, I cannot write, so that a friend, the Reverend Newman, has kindly undertaken this task for me today. After all these years, I can scarcely believe that you are alive. The Reverend Newman brought me news from The Times *of London newspaper that you and a number of others – convicts and landed gentlemen – had succeeded in a grand expedition, exploring the mountains in faraway New South Wales. My heart leapt and I cried when he told me! My own son, alive, and a famous explorer!*

But I write with tragic news; your father is dead.

William stopped reading. It was as he feared. He pressed his fingers to his eyes, as if by doing so he could somehow stop his grief, then wiped at the tears that were starting to come.

"Oh, William! I am *so* sorry, but I wanted you to read it for yourself."

William nodded, mumbling, "I understand, Mary, I do understand."

With his voice faltering, he continued to read.

When you were sent away, we lost everything. We lost your father's job and with it the lock-keeper's cottage, and from that moment we were forced to live apart and upon the parish. After you were gone, your darling father grew weaker, and quickly became a sick old man, and some ten years ago he finally departed this world; God rest his soul! He now lies peacefully in the churchyard at St James's, in the shade of the old oak, close to the graves of his own father and mother.

William covered his eyes and for the first time since the death of Whittaker cried freely. Mary said nothing but held him to her bosom, kissing the top of his head and gently stroking his hair. When he felt he could cry no more, he straightened his back and dried the tears on his cuff.

"There's more, Mary," he said. She nodded mutely, and sat down again.

I hope you are happy, and have found a good woman. I know not what more I can tell you beyond that there has not been a day when we have not thought

about you and what you are doing. Rose, Daniel, and Jane are with me now and send you their prayers and their love. My love too, as always, is with you.
Mother.

With both palms William pressed down on the letter, slowly stood up, then spoke, as much to himself as to Mary.

"Dead. He's been dead for *ten* years. All this time, Mary, and I did not know that my own father was dead!"

"How *were* you to know, Will?" Mary whispered, "Who knows what else has happened beyond these shores? None of it was your fault."

William walked to the window, leaving the letter on the table, bathed in the flickering light of the oil-lamp. He pressed his face to the pane – as he had often done as a child – and looked up to the distant stars. The sky was black and clear, and in the silence, he was transported, to a time before Australia, before the trial, before the fight at the lock and Adam's untimely death in the cold waters of the Hensford canal. He was a boy again, arm in arm with his father – his mother, brother, and sisters standing expectantly to the side, their excitement almost too much for them to contain. The sun was shining as they turned the key and pushed opened the door to the lock-keeper's cottage, their new home, the future stretching out like the silver ribbon of the canal that they had done so much to construct.

William turned away from the window, and after a moment of hesitation, spoke quietly into the gloom,

"We're going home Mary. We are going back to England."

33

Neither of them had slept well when William woke to find Billy standing at the foot of the bed.

"What's this?" Billy asked, holding up his father's bloodied shirt.

Mary jumped out of bed and grabbed the shirt from her son.

"Will? What happened? It's covered in blood. And your face, it looks like you were…Will, what happened?"

William sat up, the aches of the previous evening's activities just starting to surface.

"Papa got hit in the face unloading the wagon, Billy. As you can see, I'm fine and will live to see another day."

Mary turned to look at William, holding her stare.

"Billy, be a good boy and go and feed *Copper*. You know where to find his oats, don't you?"

"Of *course* I do Mama. I'm not a baby," he said, then skipped out of the bedroom.

"'Unloading the wagon'?" said Mary, then came to sit on the bed. "Must have been a hard piece of wool, Will."

"Can we talk about it later, Mary? I think we should be thinking about the letter."

Mary leaned into him and kissed him tenderly on the cheek, being careful not to press too hard.

"I just worry about you, that's all."

She stood up and held out the shirt at arm's length. "I'll put this in the tub and make us something to eat."

When they had eaten, Mary came back to the table and sat next to William. He was staring into the distance, red filling his eyes.

"Are you ready to talk?" she asked.

He nodded.

"It's my family. Living on the parish. My father and mother always worked hard, never asked anybody for anything. I can't bear to think how they must have lived since I left, and," he wiped away the tears, "it *is* my fault."

She took his hands in hers.

"It's *not*, Will. It's not your fault, or my fault, or your family's fault. It's the fault of the system. It's cruel and barbaric and rips us apart from the ones we love and…" she struggled to find the right words, "and it spewed us up, months later, here, on the other side of the world. What were you to do? You were abandoned. We all were."

For a long moment, he sat, looking down, allowing Mary's words to settle. He knew she was right, but the pain of his father's death, and the plight of his family, still wrenched at his heart.

"I'm the eldest son, and I've got to get back and help them." He looked up. "We can leave Gumtree in charge of the farm. I'd trust him with my life, and what he does not know about Merinos is not worth knowing."

Another long moment passed, neither of them speaking.

"Can we afford it, Will?" Mary asked quietly, fiddling with her ring. "Have we the money? Where would we live? And what about Billy and Annie?"

He pushed back his hair and sat up straighter, squaring his shoulders.

"We can find the money, especially now, after yesterday's sales. And there must be a way for Gumtree to send us money. I don't know how, but it must be possible. We could stay with your family, maybe – in London – until we were ready to move on. To Hensford. Couldn't we, Mary? Just for a few weeks – a month, maybe?"

"Maybe," she said. "But I don't really know if my mother and father are dead or alive. Last time I saw them we were all living in Spitalfields, but now?" she shrugged her shoulders, "I just don't know."

By the end of the afternoon, William had visited Blaxland, told him his news, and the plans he had for Gumtree and his farm. The older man had poured them both a brandy, and wishing him God's speed and all good fortune, looked him squarely in the eye, and reminded him that his present adventure was far from over.

"There's a need for good men such as you here, William. Never say never, and please return to finish what you started. However, I can help you when you arrive in England." He took out his pen, wrote rapidly for a few moments, then folded the paper over and added a wax seal. "Here. Take this letter and present it to my bank in London," he said. "It allows you an initial sum, and then a fixed amount monthly. I will reimburse myself from the profits of the farm." Then sighing, added, "Promise me you'll come back."

William pocketed the letter carefully and thanked him for the trust he had shown in him, and for giving him the chance to start his life anew. Then he made his way down to the stables where he knew he would find Galvin.

The tangerine sky was streaked with gold, the heat of the afternoon starting to subside, when William found his friend sitting in the yard, enjoying the last pipe of the day.

"Will, me ol'fellah! What brings you to these parts? I thought you'd be on your veranda, watching the sun go down at the end of a hard day's graft."

"Sean. It's good to see you. But I've come with some news."

Galvin looked serious.

"News? Nothing bad I hope."

William took a deep breath. "I learned yesterday that my father is dead – ten years since – and my family – well – they are destitute and living on the parish."

Galvin stood up, took off his hat and laid his pipe to one side. "Will, I don't know what to say."

"There *is* nothing you can say, Sean; but thank-you all the same. What's done is done, but," he hesitated before continuing, "we, the family and me, are going back to England. As soon as we can."

"Jaysus, that's as bad a piece of news as ever I have heard," he said, before hugging William. They stood, arms around each other, for a full half-minute before Galvin pulled away and, shoving William's hat hard down onto his head again, told him that he would just have to find himself a new best mate.

"But that won't be easy, my friend, not after what we went through in the mountains," he added.

William nodded, and smiled at the memory. "I have a favour to ask of you, Sean."

"You want me to come too? I'd love to, but I have far too much to do here."

"You'd be very welcome Sean, of course, but what I really want you to do," he said, his voice starting to break, "is to look after *Copper,* to *have* him, and to make sure he has a long and happy retirement. And most of all, to stop those bloody flies from tormenting the old boy!" he added, managing a small laugh.

Galvin stood to attention and raised his hand in a salute.

"William Parker, nothing would give me greater pleasure. It would be an honour and a privilege."

When he got home, the children were asleep and the house quiet. Mary, sitting outside and sewing, looked up.

"I told Billy, just like you asked," she said.

"What did he say?"

"Not much. Then wanted to know if we would see The King, and what would happen to *Copper.*" Mary placed her sewing in her lap and held out her hand for William to take.

"And you? What did Blaxland say? And did you see Sean?"

"I saw both, as I had hoped. Gregory, of course, was sad to see us go, and made me promise to return."

"And did you, Will? Promise to return?"

"I nodded, but promised nothing. And Sean, he has promised to take good care of *Copper.* So, Billy can be sure that he'll be well looked after, and can have an easier time in his retirement."

"That's good," said Mary and pulled him in closer. "Do you know what my grandma always used to tell us? 'Where one door closes, another opens.' Now, I'm tired Will; take me to bed."

34

They had left early that morning, before sunrise, Mary and the children travelling in a chaise driven by Blaxland's driver, William trotting alongside on *Copper.* The children quickly fell asleep, and remained so as they left behind the place they had made their home. They reached Parramatta just after daybreak, William paying the gatekeeper before they were allowed to follow the toll-road east towards Sydney, from where they would be leaving later that day.

On their right, the river pointed them in the direction of the sea and was already busy with the small craft that plied their way daily between the wharves of the town and Sydney's bustling quayside some fifteen miles away.

By noon, they had reached Cockle Creek, on Sydney's southern edge, and were starting to traverse the brickfields. A group of convicts stopped work to watch them roll by. They were toiling in clay, up to their knees in water, much as William had done the year before they left; his mind turned to the day he'd decided, following that encouraging wave from the banks of the Tank Stream, that he should ask Mary to become his wife.

"Mary!" he shouted, "Do you remember this place?"

"I remember you kissing me, covering me in clay, then a few weeks later me saying 'yes', if that's what you mean," she shouted back with a smile.

Another group of convicts, marching in line with feet chained together, crossed the family's path. None raised his head, but merely followed the criminal in front, hand upon his shoulder – each man in his own private prison.

The carriage trundled on, towards the ships whose towering masts could now be seen fringing the town's northern horizon. The place had grown since they were last here. William noted the additions: a new gallows, windmills, an extra spire here and there, and in the churchyard, scores of fresh graves. But of all the changes, one stood out, above the rest, and made Sydney appear to William like a place he'd never seen before: he and Mary were free. Free to stop and gawp, to pass the time of day with whomsoever they wished, to window-shop, to buy, or not to buy, to dawdle, without a backward glance over their shoulders. They were free of a convict's fear. They turned onto Pitt Street, passing their first home; and the flag still flew proud over Government House.

Passing the junction to Bridge Street, William was suddenly aware of the sound of the docks, and for the first time that day, it truly dawned on him – they *were* actually leaving. They were leaving a place that had at first seemed like another world, with its strange animals and multi-coloured birds; leaving an ancient place where everything was new, a place where you needed your friends, but nobody could be trusted; but above all a place they now regarded as home, and the only one their children had ever known.

When they arrived at Campbell's Wharf, the others were waiting. Gumtree and Galvin were chatting while Blaxland sat a short distance away, his head in a book. All around them, men and boys were scurrying, pushing handcarts, rolling barrels and lifting bales, carrying sacks of wool, and crates of provisions for the long journey ahead. The quayside rang with the sound of hooves and wheels, and everywhere, it seemed, people were shouting, swearing, giving or taking orders, angry conversations criss-crossing the dockside. Billy stood in the carriage, his mouth agape.

"What's *that* Mama?" he asked, pointing to the ship making ready to depart, moored in the centre of the cove.

"That, young man, is the *Sydney Packet*, the ship that is going to take us all the way to England."

"But Mama, it's *so* big!"

"It's a very long way to England, Billy," Mary explained gently, "and it's got places for us to sleep, for animals, and for all the things we're taking with us, too."

While Billy continued to gawp, Mary held up his baby sister, to look at the ship that would take them home, if home were what it proved to be.

Billy looked down at his feet. "Has it room for *Copper*, too?" he said quietly.

Mary reached out and hugged him.

"No Billy. As we have told you, *Copper* is old and would not like to be at sea for such a long time. Think – where would he be able to run on-board? And where could he find fresh grass to eat?"

Billy nodded silently; his head still bowed.

William dismounted, tethered *Copper*, then walked over to where his friends were waiting.

"Gumtree, Sean," he said, shaking each by the hand, "it's good of you to come."

"Sure, we couldn't let you sneak away just like *that*," Galvin said, with a wink.

"And besides, you've still got the keys to your storehouse," added Gumtree, "and we couldn't wait till you came back to get the wool sorted and to market. Someday, you're going to need the money."

"So," William said, looking across at the three-master, its sails still furled, "this is it. I can't believe it has really come to pass. Never thought the day would really come…" his voice trailed off.

"William!" Blaxland had closed his book and was striding towards them. He pointed at the sky. "The wind's picking up. A fair day for a voyage, but one I wished never to see."

William greeted his former boss, while Gumtree and Galvin touched their hats and backed away, to stand a little way off.

"Are you ready to go, m'boy? And what of Mary? And little Billy," he whispered, the concern in his voice clear to William. "Does he understand what's happening?"

"As much as he can, Gregory, but the real test will be when we lose sight of land. He's never been on a ship before, so we can but pray."

"Indeed," Blaxland nodded, and smiled sadly. "We are all going to miss you, you know."

"I know, Gregory, I know," said William, summoning a smile.

"Well, there's much to be done, so we had best leave you to it. If Mary and the little ones are ready, I will take the carriage back; and I'll drop off Gumtree en-route to South Creek. Galvin, I believe, is taking *Copper*. Am I correct?"

"Yes, you are, Gregory. He's promised to look after him as one of his own, and I know he will," said William, then turned and walked over to where Mary was still hugging Billy.

"He's a bit upset about *Copper*," she explained in a whisper.

"Right; well, it's time to say our goodbyes and make sure all our things are loaded." He held out his hand and helped Mary and Lizzie down from the chaise, leaving Billy to jump from the step and follow them, running over to where the three men stood talking.

William bade his friends farewell, and as Mary said her last goodbyes – the faintest of blushes colouring her cheek as Galvin took her hand – he walked unnoticed over to *Copper*. The horse raised his head in recognition.

"*Copper*," William said quietly, "you are my dearest friend." Taking his huge head in his hands, he held him close, rocking gently from side to side. "What am I to do without you? But Sean – Sean will take good care of you. I know he will. And if we ever come back, it will be you I visit first – I promise."

He took a step back and looked deep into the horse's eyes.

Then taking his head once more into his arms, he whispered, "I love you," turned around, and walked away, towards the longboat waiting to carry them to their ship.

He did not turn to face the land until he and the family were safely on-board the *Packet*.

35

By now, their attention was beginning to turn away from the quayside to the activities onboard. Billy watched, fascinated, as cartload after cartload rumbled its way across the quay, including, he noted, a number carrying pigs, sheep, and bleating goats, all of which were transferred first into the waiting longboats and then into the bowels of the vessel itself. All around them, scores of sailors worked furiously to get the voyage underway. Alarmed at hearing cries from above, Billy strained to watch the men moving around the rigging – they were tiny against the sky, scurrying like rats up the masts, or dangling from the spars, their faraway shouts carried away on the breeze.

Looking back towards the quay, there was now no sign of the others – they were either lost among a sea of carts and carriages, or long-gone and hidden behind the sprawl of timber yards and warehouses that made up Campbell's Wharf. Mary leant into

William, shielding herself against the chill breeze beginning to rise. Following his gaze, she joined him in scanning the distant scene, then said, "They were good friends, weren't they, Will? Stood by you, through thick and thin."

William said nothing, but nodded, and carried on staring silently across the water, watching the windmills, set high on the cliffs at Miller's Point – the slow turn of their sails seeming to count down their few remaining minutes. Finally, he spoke. "You're right Mary," he said, "we're leaving it all in safe hands." She smiled, kissed his cheeks, then straightened his collar.

Suddenly, she stopped and looked down, her eyes fixed on his chest.

"Will?"

"What?"

"You never told me; the morning after the letter arrived, why your shirt was covered in blood."

William pursed his lips, then took her head gently in his hands.

"I didn't want to upset you, Mary. And besides, we had just found out that my father had died."

"Yes, but I still want to know. It wasn't an accident, was it?"

He paused.

"No, not an accident. It was Gates, Tommy Gates, who hit me."

Mary put her hand to her mouth.

"*Gates!* He *knew* where we lived?"

William pulled her into him, speaking close to her ear.

"No, like me, he was visiting the market, so just a coincidence. And he won't remember anything of the evening. He was already in his cups when Gumtree poleaxed him – laid him flat out on the floor of The Mason's. He's gone Mary. History." He paused, then stepping back, he said firmly, "It won't be long before we depart. Let's get ourselves ready."

They went below decks to show Billy their cabin, then swiftly returned to the fo'c'sle. Mary gripped Billy's hand and held Lizzie close as all about, gangs of sailors rushed back and forth making ready to leave. High above, men continued to prepare the sails, whilst another group clustered around the giant capstan, fitted the long wooden bars into place, then got into position, waiting for the order to weigh anchor. They did not have long to wait. On the word, the shantyman got the manoeuvre started, singing loudly:

Come breast the bars, bullies, heave her away,
Weigh hey, roll and go!
Soon we'll be rolling her down through the Bay,
To be rollicking randy dandy-O!'

to which, as one, the men replied:

Heave a pawl, O heave away!
Weigh hey, roll and go!
The anchor's on board and the cable's all stored,
To be rollicking randy dandy-O!

As the sailors' bare feet stamped forward in slow unison, and the rope, creaking under the strain, inched the anchor off the harbour floor, Billy put his fingers in his ears and watched, mesmerised by the slow turn of the capstan. When the anchor was finally secured, another order saw a pair of longboats begin to pull the ship gradually out towards deeper water, out between the gun batteries standing guard at the entrance to the cove.

Slowly, but surely, they were leaving Sydney.

While his family looked to the front, William lent against the bulwark and faced backwards, towards the town. And as the ship ploughed on, he allowed his thoughts to drift back over the years since he and Mary first set foot on the blood-red soil of Australia. Like the leaves of a book, turned by the wind, they flipped past his eyes, each page met by an involuntary smile, a grimace, or the raising of an eyebrow. Then, without warning, his thoughts turned to the future, to the long journey ahead, with its storms and dangers that would lurk, unseen, beneath the surface; and to England, to Hensford, and to the Clarkes, within whose welcoming bosom they certainly would not be embraced.

An urgent tug at his sleeve broke his reverie.

He saw Billy looking up at him, frowning, hands on hips.

"Papa? I *asked* you! Is that England – over *there?*"

"What?" William returned to the present. Shielding his eyes, he peered across the glittering blues of the South Seas, towards a tiny speck of land, even now disappearing behind a curtain of grey, sweeping the smudged line of the distant horizon.

"That island over there? No, Billy, we have a *long* way to go yet, before we get to England."

Billy continued to frown.

"But what will it be *like*, papa?"

William thought, then said, "Well Billy, the sun is kind, the rainfall soft, and the grass…the grass is of the purest green – the colour of your mother's eyes."

William looked at Mary, swaddling Lizzie to her breast, and was pleased to see her blush.

But still, the boy was not satisfied.

"But, Papa, how will I *know*? How can I be *sure* it's England?"

William crouched down and laid his arm gently across his son's shoulders.

"You just will, Billy," he said, his eyes beginning to redden.

"I promise you.

You just will."

THE END

Author's Note

The Land Beyond the Seas depicts some historical events that actually happened and includes some characters who did live in the fledgling country that was Australia in the early nineteenth century. However, it is first and foremost a work of fiction so that most characters and most events are figments of my imagination, and a certain amount of artistic licence has also been taken with what remains including, and especially, the journey through the Blue Mountains. If readers would like to know more about this expedition, then *The Journal of Gregory Blaxland 1813* would be a good place to start.

As for other aspects of life in the colony at this time, I would recommend the following books and sources:

Watkin Tench 1788 (introduced by Tim Flannery)

The Fatal Shore by Robert Hughes

The Story of Australia by AGL Shaw

The Colony – A History of Early Sydney by Grace Karskens

In addition, the Sydney Living Museums, The Australian Dictionary of Biography, The State Library of New South Wales, *The Sydney Gazette* and, last but not least, Wikipedia have all proven to be rich sources of useful information.